DATE DUE

Jun 29 '82	Aug 6 85		
Aug 4 '82			
Aug 23 '82			
Aug 31 '8	WITHDRAWN		
Jan 11 '83			
Jan 28 '83			
Feb 4 '83			
Feb 26 '8			
Apr 4 '83			
Apr 26 '83			

F
War

Warner, Mignon
Death in time

Death in Time

By Mignon Warner

Death in Time

MIGNON WARNER

PUBLISHED FOR THE CRIME CLUB BY

DOUBLEDAY & COMPANY, INC.

GARDEN CITY, NEW YORK

1982

All of the characters in this book
are fictitious, and any resemblance
to actual persons, living or dead,
is purely coincidental.

Library of Congress Cataloging in Publication Data

Warner, Mignon.
Death in time.

I. Title.
PR6073.A7275D4   823'.914
ISBN 0-385-18094-2   AACR2
Library of Congress Catalog Card Number 81-43766
Copyright © 1982 by Mignon Warner
All Rights Reserved
Printed in the United States of America
First Edition

CHAPTER 1

It never failed to surprise and delight Nigel Playford, the suddenness with which the lush green Welsh landscape asserted itself and declared its total independence of character and personality from the depressing industrial Midlands through which he and his sister had passed that afternoon. A long drive. Four hours it had taken them—over half an hour of that wasted, thanks to Cynthia's poor navigation driving round in circles in the East End of London. They hadn't spoken since then. Correction: Cynthia had inquired whether he was driving with the hand brake on. That must have been somewhere near the Coventry turnoff. An hour ago, maybe a bit more. Sarcasm, of course. Cynthia was very bitchy today. Bitchier than usual, that is. He had often wondered what her first spoken words were. . . . A criticism of some kind, he felt sure. Probably some comment concerning her own physical comfort and general wellbeing. Her lack thereof, he amended.

A vague feeling of uneasiness came over him. He hoped the hotel wouldn't be too primitive. That would be the last straw. . . . Last February in Blackpool all over again. Cyn would storm out of the hotel and take the first train back to London. She hadn't really wanted to come in the first place; so she would be looking for anything, the slightest excuse, and she would stalk out on him, just as she had in February (and that had been a five-star hotel; this was only a three!). This time maybe it would be for good. Once she married Dr. Henry Beamish—*if* she married Henry Beamish; or rather, if Henry's wife *let* Henry marry her—that was it, the finish. . . .

Frowning slightly, Nigel concentrated his thoughts on the rap-

idly changing scenery. Why let that supercilious bastard
Beamish spoil the weekend?

They were driving now along the wide sweep of coastal road
which would take them to Plaid-yro-Wyth, their destination—a
small seaside resort dominated by Great Mountain which gave
the town its name and brooded over it like some stern, uncom-
promising paterfamilias.

Nigel ducked his head and glanced up through the slush-
speckled windscreen. Somewhere out there to their right was
Snowdon, lost in the distance in heavy mist and yet somehow
much nearer at hand, right on top of them, so that one was always conscious of its presence even though one could not actually see it. He shivered a little and turned up the heating. It was
getting dark and raining lightly, and from the haunted look
about the odd few people whom he had observed scurrying on
foot about their business, very cold. (*Please God, let there be
nothing wrong with The Grand's central-heating system: Cyn
will go mad!*)

Where had that happened to them before? Trouble with the
central heating. . . . Eighteen months ago at Brighton, wasn't it?
No, more recently than that: Hastings last October. The *I*er
Euro Congrès de Magie. (Why the organisers hadn't been able
to come up with something appropriate in English was beyond
him: of the seven hundred and thirty registrants at the convention, no more than one tenth spoke French, if that!)

A malicious smile drew back the corners of his wide mouth,
thinning it so that now it seemed to stretch from ear to ear. It
made his unlined, podgy pink-and-white face with its deep-set
eyes look more than ever like that of a ventriloquist's dummy, all
mouth. No, the problem at Brighton had been far more spectacular than a spot of bother with a cantankerous central-heating
boiler which kept blowing up. It had started with the banquet—
the usual uninspired saddle of lamb and green garden peas—and
reached its climax with the after-banquet floor show. Not the
cabaret—the programmed entertainment, he smiled to himself
(that had been nowhere near as entertaining!)—but the unsched-

uled floor show which had got under way during coffee and li-
queurs. He hadn't thought it so terribly entertaining then, of
course. At the time he hadn't thought anything at all. Too
shocked. Not by Cyn's behaviour. It had been pretty tame stuff
compared with some of the rages he'd seen her work herself into
when she was a kid. It was Kath Sexton who had taken his
breath away. Everyone's! She had completely lost control. Let
go. Would've killed Cyn if they hadn't dragged the two of them
apart. They'd been like a pair of mad dogs, oblivious to everything and everyone but themselves and their intense mutual
hatred for one another.

He chuckled to himself. The look of surprise on Cyn's face
when Kath jumped up from the table, sending her half-filled
coffee cup flying, and her chair (which had got broken in the
melee that followed), and went for her. Never thought Kath had
it in her. Cyn had expected Kath to put up a fight for Frank, but
with her cheque-book not with her fists and feet. (God, he'd
never seen anything like it!) Cyn had slipped up badly there; but
then Cyn had always underestimated people. She'd always been
short on appreciation for how the other person felt. She didn't
care what anyone else felt. Cyn had only ever cared about Cyn.
How Cyn felt. In a way it was a kind of contempt. People only
ever get what they deserve. . . . That was her usual line of
defence. If Kath Sexton had been prepared to sit back and put
up with her husband's having an affair with another woman,
then that was her funeral.

But Kath hadn't sat back. For the best part of a year, maybe;
but then *wham!* And Cyn hadn't known what had hit her.

"You're smirking," remarked Cynthia Playford coldly, without
looking at her brother. "Can't I share the joke?"

"You wouldn't appreciate it," he replied, turning his head to
grin at her.

Cynthia sucked in her breath and let it out in a sharp hiss.
"Look out! The lights have changed."

He jerked his head to the front but it was too late. They were
already over the crossing, the ruffled, highly indignant look on

the face of the pedestrian who glared after them suggesting that he might've just had an encounter of the very unpleasant kind.

"That makes the fifth set of pedestrian traffic lights you've driven straight through on red today," his sister pointed out icily. "They're there for a reason, you know."

He flicked his eyes over the side of her face, then took a slightly longer, more thoughtful look at her. The china-doll complexion was even more fragile, transparent almost, tinged with grey round her mouth and nostrils and eyes. The tragically doomed consumptive heroine of a romantic Victorian novel! Something to do with the poor light? She looked nearer forty-eight than thirty-eight. Her hair wasn't right, either. Lank, mousy, not the usual fluffy pale white-gold halo that set off those exquisitely delicate features which he had always found so fascinating. She had a cruel mouth, wide and thin like his, but he had never noticed that, on himself or on her. In his eyes she was physical perfection, a curious notion he also entertained about himself.

"What's wrong?" he asked impulsively. An observation made subconsciously several days earlier put the words in his mouth before he had had time to ponder the wisdom of such an inquiry. Cynthia was easily irritated, particularly by this line of questioning.

"What d'you mean, *what's wrong?*" she mimicked him, sneering. Scowling, she opened her large brown leather shoulder bag and gazed into it. "Nothing's wrong."

He looked sideways at her. She was still gazing into the shoulder bag, almost as if trying to remember what it was that she had wanted from it. He glanced down, wondered what was in the bulky envelope which was wedged lengthwise between her black leather-bound appointment diary and her money wallet, but knew better than to ask. "The good doctor having second thoughts?" he inquired after a moment.

Cynthia's right hand disappeared between the envelope and her diary and re-emerged a few seconds later with a small, clear plastic pill container. She popped one of the pills, Valium, into her mouth, tossing back her head as she swallowed it. Then, clenching her teeth until her jaw ached, she glowered out of the side window and muttered, "Mind your own damned business!"

Nigel glanced at her. Something about her voice, her expression. . . . His heart gave a dull thud, paused, then fluttered against his rib cage. He could hardly keep his excitement out of his voice. "It's all over, isn't it? Between you and good old Henry?"

Cynthia ignored him.

"His old lady turned nasty?"

Cynthia's head swung round and her light green eyes blazed at him. He braced himself, but the accompanying lashing he expected from her tongue never materialised and it was a moment or two before he realised what was holding her back. The sinews of her neck gave her away. They were standing out like fine cords. Cynthia couldn't speak; she was too overcome with emotion. He wasn't sure what kind, but white-hot rage was high on his list of possibilities. Cyn had a devil of a temper.

Her eyes suddenly misted over and she looked quickly away.

"No," she said at length. "As a matter of fact she didn't. I finished it."

He gave her a quick look and let out a derisive hoot. "That'll be the day! You've never ended an affair in your whole life. It's not your style—now is it, darling? Be honest. Always the married man with the clinging, well-heeled little woman hovering in the background wringing her hands in despair." He narrowed his eyes at the shiny black strip of road ahead of them. "I've never been able to figure it out, Cyn, who it is you really hate. Men or women. Father, Mother? Yourself? Is it you you want to hurt? Is that why you always get mixed up in these hopeless triangles?"

Cynthia said dully, "Rita Beamish is dying. Six months, that's all she's got. Probably less."

"Since when?" he asked disbelievingly.

Her head swung round, eyes ablaze. "She's dying, damn you!"

"Language," he said mildly. He hesitated, considered the implications of Mrs. Henry Beamish's imminent demise, whether it was even true that she was dying. Maybe good old Henry was pulling a fast one on Cyn, using his wife's ill health as his escape clause; pronouncing his wife incurably ill and then coming up with a miracle cure. After he'd got shot of Cynthia, of course, leaving it to her to do the decent thing in the circumstances and bow out gracefully. No scenes. A fond farewell and a stiff upper lip. . . .

Nigel decided tentatively, for argument's sake, to accept Cynthia's claim at face value. "So that's it, eh?" he said slowly. "The best-laid plans and all that. This time your victim (you'll pardon me for calling him that!) is free and unencumbered. As good as. My God, that must've put the breeze up you, Cyn . . . when good old Henry told you about his wife and you realised that this time you were lumbered, that soon there'd be no little woman around to get you off the hook."

"No," she said after a small pause. "I'm sorry to disappoint you, Nigel, but it wasn't like that at all." She twisted round slightly in her seat to look at her brother; there was a faintly triumphant gleam in her eye. "Henry Beamish is the only man I've ever really loved."

Her eyes held her brother's for a very long moment; and then, smiling as if she had scored a very great personal triumph, she settled back in her seat and looked again to the front.

CHAPTER 2

A slim white plastic arrow on the black velvet notice board in reception indicated the way to the ballroom. Neat lines of tiny white plastic lettering spelt out the further information that in this, the ballroom, and in the Marlborough Room (the latter open for registration at 10:30 A.M., Saturday), the Mystic Circle was holding its Easter Fiesta.

Nigel Playford, as a past president of the society and after having checked with his local reference library on the dictionary definition of the Spanish word *fiesta*, had objected most strongly to its use in connection with a two-day magicians' convention. This was no *saint's day* they were celebrating (though in his pique over the matter he had wryly remarked to his sister that it wouldn't surprise him one little bit if in the event the weekend fiesta turned out to be in honour of her old flame, St. Frank Sexton!).

Nigel was told not to be so bloody pedantic (by Frank Sexton, naturally, whose brainchild it was—incubated, Nigel had no doubt, during a recent package holiday Sexton had taken on the Costa Brava) and that having taken the trouble to look up the word, he would also undoubtedly know that it could be used quite properly in connection with any kind of joyful celebration or festival (of magic, in this instance); and ultimately the motion was seconded, carried, and duly recorded in the society's minute book. *Fiesta* it was and looked like remaining. That was if the weekend were a success and it were decided by the committee to make an annual event of it.

"Bloody ridiculous!" muttered Nigel as he plonked his and his sister's suitcases to one side of the notice board and the offend-

ing noun blasted him squarely between the eyes. "With Sexton
having a say in things they mean *siesta,* don't they?"

He looked round when there was no response from his sister
and saw that she was wandering up and down the wide, thickly
carpeted gallerylike corridor to the right of the reception desk
looking at the luxury goods in the display cases which decorated
the green and gold flock-papered walls. He beckoned to her, but
she blandly ignored him and carried on with her tour of inspec-
tion, disappearing a moment later into what, according to a narrow lacquered-wood sign affixed to the wall farther along from
the desk, was the Wellington Room.

Nigel cursed mildly under his breath as he picked up the pen
to register. So this was how it was going to be, was it? Charming,
bloody charming!

"Just arrived, eh?"

Nigel turned to the voice. A slim, middle-aged man with a
deep, artificially maintained tan and a defensive air was eyeing
him speculatively.

"Uh? Oh," said Nigel, without much enthusiasm. "Hullo,
Frank. Yes, we've only just arrived. Late starting out," he mumbled, looking round vaguely for the porter.

"If you'd like to go on up to your room, Mr. Playford,"
suggested the pretty young blonde behind the desk, acknowl-
edging Frank Sexton with a pert smile of recognition, "I'll get
the porter to take your things up as soon as he's free. He should
only be a moment."

Nigel nodded and stood aside, allowing several new arrivals
for the weekend whom he knew slightly and had greeted with a
perfunctory smile and a quick nod of the head to move up to the
desk and register.

"Time for a drink before you go up?" inquired Sexton hesitantly. "Tea, if you'd prefer it. I believe they're serving it now in
the Wellington Room. Kath went on ahead."

Nigel glanced quickly along the corridor in some alarm, but
his panic was only momentary. There was no sign of Cynthia either plastered up against the wall or lying spattered in little bits

all over the carpet, so her confrontration with Kath Sexton—their first meeting since the Brighton fiasco eighteen months ago—had gone off without incident. That was if Kath were in the Wellington Room. Maybe she'd changed her mind about afternoon tea and had gone out for a walk instead. . . .

Curiosity prompted Nigel's acceptance of Sexton's invitation rather than any real desire to take some kind of refreshment with him. He didn't like Sexton, never had, and sometimes—like now when Cynthia was going out of her way to be difficult and he could see they were in for a trying weekend—it was hard not to let it show. The man was a self-centred, humourless, youth-fixated bore: the worst kind of know-it-all, the type who actually does know what he is talking about and is never wrong. Nigel didn't even bother to live in hopes on that score. Frank Sexton was the world's foremost authority on magic and magicians and the allied arts and always would be, for the remainder of his life-time and long after his death, if not for all time because of his extensive writings on all three subjects. In the pecking order of who knew the most and was held in highest esteem for that knowledge, Nigel came in a poor second. But Nigel didn't let it depress him. In fact it was a constant source of satisfaction and comfort to him. He had reached his position without even trying, whereas Sexton had devoted his every waking moment (latterly, that is) to getting to the top and making sure that he stayed there.

"It's what comes of being a nobody in everyday life," Nigel had remarked in a sneering aside to his sister after he had first introduced Sexton to her and Sexton had moved away. "Let it be a warning to you!"

"What does he do for a living?" Cynthia had asked in a whisper, eyeing Sexton's departing back with some interest.

"Chairman of the board of directors of one of the smaller building societies," Nigel had responded in kind, whereupon Cynthia had given him one of her withering looks; and then, in that bone-dry voice which he knew so well, she had said, "Oh yes, I see what you mean. On a salary of between twenty and thirty thousand quid per annum, definitely one of life's failures."

Nigel had tried, not too successfully with that wide, gaping mouth of his, to conceal his amusement. He had always been able to count on Cynthia to rise to the bait.

"He's retired," he had said, staring fixedly at the floor (if he had looked directly at her he definitely wouldn't have been able to keep a straight face).

"Rubbish," she had shot back at him. "He's no more than forty-five—fifty at most."

"Okay, so I was being kind." Nigel had, at this point, been unable to help himself: he had had to smile. "Sexton's chief accountant had his hand in the till . . . fed a long string of phoney accounts into the computer. Took the whole board of directors down the drain with him . . . very nearly the whole show, in fact."

And that, in Nigel's opinion, had been the beginning of the affair: the researcher's passion—and Cynthia was one of the best authors' researchers around—for all the facts.

She had never said, but over the twelve months that the affair had lasted, she must have compiled quite an intimate biographical dossier on Frank Sexton. Or if she hadn't, then she could if asked to—assuming, of course, that there was someone about who would find Sexton and his cohorts sufficiently interesting to warrant the writing of a book on the £1.5-million swindle which had precipitated their collective downfall, and needed all the pertinent facts and figures.

Again Cynthia had never said—and Nigel hadn't asked—but she probably even had a pretty shrewd idea whether or not it were true that Sexton and others on the board were co-conspirators and as guilty of fraud (something that had only ever been hinted at) as the building society's chief accountant. Fortunately for Sexton, and for anyone else whom it might have concerned, the chief accountant had very obligingly suffered a fatal coronary while the matter was under investigation; and so the full extent of the swindle, whether he had been alone in the conspiracy to defraud, had died with him. And/or, Nigel had heard it rumoured (because the fraud had been a particularly complex and sophisticated one and therefore difficult if not impossible to explain to a jury of laymen with no technical knowledge of computers), had been swept neatly under the carpet by the powers-that-be.

Nigel went on slowly ahead of Sexton, who had excused himself for a moment while he had a quick word with the receptionist, something to do with a raincoat which had gone missing —whose Nigel wasn't sure; he wasn't that interested. Sexton caught up with him at the mahogany and glass swing doors which gave onto the Wellington Room. Nigel was peering intently through the glass, searching the scattering of armchairs and settees beyond, not for Sexton's wife, as Sexton incorrectly surmised a second or two later, but for Cynthia. Nigel couldn't see her anywhere. Several other familiar faces, but not hers.

Holding open the door for Nigel, Sexton gestured with his head. "There's Kath, over by that marble pillar."

Sexton hesitated; looked uncomfortable. The broad-beamed waitress who had bent over to place a tea tray before his wife had straightened up and moved on to take an order from another table, giving the two men standing at the door their first unobstructed view of the woman sitting with Kath Sexton.

"Oh—" said Sexton abruptly. The door swung silently closed behind him. He continued to hesitate and seemed undecided about something, as if he were having second thoughts about his invitation or had suddenly remembered some other, more pressing business that required his immediate attention elsewhere. Then, in a flat voice: "Cynthia."

"Yes," said Nigel, smiling. He led the way across the room, weaving deftly in and out of the haphazardly arranged tables and chairs. Then, shooting a quick backwards glance at Sexton, all innocence but thoroughly enjoying every moment of Sexton's fairly obvious disconcertion: "I did mention that I'd brought Cyn along with me, didn't I?"

Sexton frowned at Nigel's back. "I thought she said she'd

never come to another convention after the treatment she got at that hotel you stayed at in Blackpool last February."

"Oh, you know Cyn," replied Nigel casually, smiling briefly and then saying, "Hullo, nice to see you again; how are you?" to someone he knew.

Drawing nearer to the two women, who were taking tea together, Sexton wiped the frown off his face and put on an uneasy smile.

His fears—and he had them, not half an hour since his wife had warned him what she would do to Cynthia Playford if she dared to show her face that weekend—were (hopefully) groundless. Cynthia and Kath were talking guardedly but amicably enough about (of all things in the circumstances, thought Sexton irritably as he drew up a chair alongside his wife and sat down) the lingerie in one of the display cases outside. He hadn't paid particular attention to any of it himself: in fact it had only vaguely registered with him that there were display cases out there; but from a certain gleam in Cynthia's eyes—the kind that made him wish he were anyplace but there—he rather gathered that there were definite similarities between a dove-grey satin negligee which both women had individually paused to admire and one which Cynthia had received as a gift several Christmases ago.

It was difficult to tell for certain (except for that one memorable occasion at Brighton!)—Kath, when she wanted to, could be extremely clever at concealing her true thoughts and feelings—but he guessed that his wife was in no doubt, as Cynthia had intended, about who the giver of that gift had been.

Sexton's stomach muscles tightened, and he drew himself tensely towards the edge of his seat, almost as if ready to spring into action should anything untoward take place. He even found his eye measuring the distance between his wife and Cynthia, and actually calculated the number of moves both would have to make before they were at one another's throat. Cynthia was virtually trapped behind the coffee table with her back hard up against the windowsill in what amounted to little more than a defensive position; whereas his wife, he noted uncomfortably, was perfectly placed for a lightning attack on the jugular and a safe retreat.

Kath laughed at him about it afterwards as they were going up to their room to rest before dinner and the evening's entertainment, tentatively and somewhat jokingly referred to as the "Night-Before Party."

"You really thought I was going to go for her again, didn't you?" she said, stepping into the waiting lift ahead of him.

"Nonsense," he said briskly, depressing the button for the third floor.

She laughed lightly. "Don't tell me it was because you wanted to go to the toilet! You were rather sitting on the edge of your seat, you know, darling."

The lift doors closed and, as if by mutual consent, they fell silent and simply watched the light on the indicator panel click dispiritedly on and off at each floor. Reaching the third, the lift came to a juddering halt; then, after a long pause, the doors parted and they stepped out.

"I thought about it," admitted Kath, picking up the conversation at the door of their room. She turned and looked at her husband expectantly to provide the key. "But then that was what she wanted me to do, wasn't it? All that nonsense about negligees . . . I knew what she was really talking about, you know. I'm not that stupid."

Opening the door, he gave it a little push and she stepped past him into the room.

"Nigel told me at the last meeting that he'd definitely be coming on his own," he said. He frowned. "I wish he'd kept to his word."

"Oh, I knew he wouldn't; I knew she'd come once she found out I'd be here."

"What d'you mean?" he asked warily, closing the door and following her part of the way across the room.

She tugged the short cord on the fluorescent light over the

dressing-table mirror. "We've still got some unfinished business to get settled between us, haven't we?"

"Kathleen," he said anxiously. "Look . . . please, just ignore her. You promised me."

"Yes," she said brightly. (A touch of hysteria there?) "Just like you promised me. Till death us do part. . . . Wasn't that what the nice gentleman in the white dog-collar said?"

Sexton had paused at the foot of the twin bed nearest the door. Sighing, he lowered himself onto the chocolate-coloured candlewick bedspread. Kath watched him for a moment, until the old increasingly familiar tight band clamped itself around her chest and she began to struggle to get her breath; and then she looked quickly away, concentrating her gaze on her grey, pinched reflection in the artificially illuminated dressing-table mirror. (*A trick of the fluorescent lighting, please dear God: that sour-faced old hag surely couldn't be her?*)

Dark, haunted eyes stared relentlessly back at her, like some stranger's, someone she was seeing for the first time. "*Frank pretends he doesn't care,*" the look in the stranger's eye whispered to her, "*but don't you believe it. He still hasn't got over her, that incestuous whore. He never will. Perhaps, if something were to happen to her—*"

Kath reached down shakily for the small splay-legged dressing-table stool, drew it out, and sat down. She picked up her hairbrush, but paused before using it and examined her reflection a little more closely. No, she definitely didn't like what she could see. She used to be quite pretty. (Was it all that long ago?) She was only forty-eight. That wasn't old. Why had she aged so much faster than Frank had? It wasn't fair. He hardly showed his years, just a little silver-grey at his temples (he was like his mother there: Mrs. Sexton had scarcely a grey hair in her head, even now at seventy-eight. An hour's squash every morning, followed by the twenty-minute jog back home from the sports centre had kept him physically and mentally in peak condition. He'd always been terribly vain about his body, forever needing fresh fields of admiration and conquest. Understandable in a younger man, but the sort of thing one would have expected him to grow out of with the passing of the years and the thickening of the waistline. Not that Frank's had done much thickening. Barely two inches since they'd married. . . .

Sexton gazed dejectedly at the loosely held room key dangling from his right hand and listened to the rhythmic stroke-stroke of the hairbrush down the side of his wife's dark head. She wasn't showing it (yet), but she was working herself into a state over Cynthia. It was going to be Brighton all over again. The hairbrushing gave her away. Did she realise that?

He couldn't remember her using a hairbrush at all—certainly not to this extent—during the early years of their marriage, though perhaps she had and he simply hadn't been aware of it. Too busy with other things to notice. There hadn't really been all that much stress in their lives until they lost Lucy. That, he guessed, was when it had probably begun, this hairbrushing, stress-relieving habit of hers. That was definitely when he had first become aware of it. And it seemed to work well enough for her. Or it had in the past, though the mere fact that the hairbrushing sessions were on the increase was a good indication that the battle with her grief was still far from won. Everyone, including himself, had expected her to break down completely over Lucy, but surprisingly she hadn't. The nearest she'd ever come to it, to a complete physical and mental breakdown, was over his affair with Cynthia Playford. It was because of Lucy that Kath hadn't been able to cope with Cynthia. There had been others—before Lucy's death and Cynthia, that is—and Kath had known about them, taken it all in her stride; forgotten about them, or so it had seemed to him, as quickly as he had. But right from the beginning Cynthia had been different.

God Almighty, it was over, finished and done with—*kaput!* What did he have to do to prove it to her? It was almost as if she were out for blood and wouldn't be satisfied until she had drawn some.

"They're laughing at us, you know," Kath said softly.

Sexton raised his head sharply and their eyes met in the mirror.

"Who d'you mean?"

"Whom," she corrected him quietly. "The Playfords. He's laughing at you and she's laughing at me."

"Oh, for God's sake, Kath, give it a rest." He pitched forward onto his feet and started for the door.

"You know what they say about those two, don't you?" There was now definitely a note of hysteria in Kath's voice, but her husband didn't hear it. He was well on his way down to the bar.

CHAPTER 3

Those attending the Night-Before Party—the convention proper would not commence officially until the registration desk opened in the Marlborough Room at ten-thirty the following morning, Easter Saturday—numbered less than twenty-five, considerably fewer than had been expected to turn up, due largely (the convention organisers sincerely hoped) to the extremely bad weather which had set in late in the afternoon and caused havoc on the roads right up and down the country but particularly in the Midlands and North Wales.

The party was held in the Wellington Room, which was open that evening to all residents, most of whom, as the night wore on, attached themselves to the determinedly festal conventioneers with a quiet, unobtrusive spontaneity that was just as quietly and spontaneously accepted by their informal hosts, those who were performing close-up magic at the tables with perhaps greater enthusiasm than the more retiring conventioneer who preferred to sit and watch and let others do the entertaining. Indeed, as Lance Headley, president of the Mystic Circle and one of the convention organisers, explained to Captain James Belson, R.N. (Retired), and Mrs. Belson, who, along with their companions for the evening, a lively sixty-five-to-seventy-year-old couple, Mr. and Mrs. Arthur Toomey, had gravitated towards the conventioneers somewhere around nine, a lot of magicians would walk a hundred miles to avoid performing in front of an audience of their own kind. Magicians, Headley assured them with the wry smile of experience, were a notoriously difficult audience for another magician to entertain.

"Know all the tricks of the trade, I daresay," commented Belson, a tall, broad-shouldered man of about sixty with a public-school accent and a marked tendency, when speaking at length, to breathlessness.

Headley, a veterinary surgeon in his middle forties with greying carrot-coloured hair, an ingratiating manner, and deep-seated frustrations (he still cherished hopes of becoming a full-time professional entertainer), shook his head. "Not a bit of it. You watch," he suggested and inclined his head at a table not far from theirs whose occupants were currently being entertained with coin tricks by a jeaned, hollow-chested youth with a bad case of acne. "King Arthur's Merlin might just possibly be given a hand for appearing and then disappearing in a puff of smoke, but the average magician is lucky if he raises an eyebrow, let alone a round of applause. Magicians generally just sit and watch . . . occasionally take notes." Headley was smiling, but he wasn't joking about the notes. It had happened to him and was quite common practice amongst magicians. The better the performer, the heavier the crop of notebooks and ball-point pens one could expect to see sprouting from the laps of the audience.

The two-piece band, comprised of piano and drums, entertained in the Wellington Room every Friday and Saturday night. (It was called the "GG's," according to the silver and blue lettering on the yellowing skin of the big drum, or the "Geriatric Generation"—the drinks waiters liked to have their little joke!) The band struck up defiantly and went into the first few bars of a popular up-tempo hit tune of the forties. No one could really say they hadn't been warned. A steady, menacing drum roll followed by an ear-splintering crash of percussion had also given a reasonable hint that something important was about to happen; and so most eyes were already turned expectantly on the hitherto largely ignored, slightly raised platform across one corner of the room which served as a bandstand and which, depending on where one was sitting, was partially screened by leafy potted plants.

The melody broke off as abruptly as it had commenced, and the drummer (who also doubled as a vocalist and was beginning to feel the competition) leaned forward on his stool and said something into a whistling microphone. Only a few got the message—something about getting up and stretching the legs which, presumably, was the drummer's quaint way of asking the guests *please* to remember that the band was there and to forget magic tricks for a few minutes and dance.

The microphone continued to whistle shrilly. One or two people covered their ears with their hands and made faces, as if the drummer had suddenly been struck stone-deaf and it was therefore necessary for someone to act out in mime to him what everybody else in the room was having to endure. He made a few quick adjustments to the head of the microphone, consulted with the pianist, who beckoned to a waiter, and between the three of them, they finally came to grips with the problem. The drummer gave everybody a thumbs-up sign and a cheery smile, and then, with an elaborate flourish of his drumsticks, he and the pianist began to play.

Only one couple, at the table where the coin manipulator was working, heeded his call immediately and took to the small, circular dance floor which two of the waiters had laid bare of carpet during dinner in readiness for the evening's entertainment. "I see what you mean," said Mrs. Toomey, watching the couple on the floor. "Those two just got straight up, never so much as excused themselves." She was speaking to Headley, who usually had a good ear for regional accents and placed hers in or near Birmingham. This time he was wrong. The Toomeys came from Bradford, straight from the street markets where they had quite literally made their fortune as laborers selling women's underclothing (seconds mostly) from a decrepit-looking, canvas-covered stall. They had retired that week: the Toomeys' doctor had detected a heart murmur in Mr. Toomey that might just be serious if he didn't take things easy from now on; and this was the first holiday or break they had taken in over forty years in business together.

Headley's eyes followed the couple's gyrations round the floor: they made no attempt to dance in the more formal manner suggested by the music provided and more commonly seen on a Friday night in The Grand's Wellington Room.

"That's Nigel Playford, the television critic," he said after a moment. "Writes a column for one of the London dailies. That's his sister with him, Cynthia Playford."

"*Grrr!*" rumbled Toomey, his large moist brown eyes twinkling lecherously behind thick-lensed spectacles. "What's Playford doing here? Covering your convention for his newspaper? Going to be on the telly, eh?"

Headley said, "No. He's one of our past presidents."

"Does that mean he's a magician too?" inquired Belson, his ragged grey eyebrows raised in curiosity. "Or was it just a courtesy title?"

Headley shook his head. "No, he's a magician—dabbles in magic purely for his own amusement. He and his sister have agreed to be on the panel of judges for our competition on Sunday afternoon to find the most promising magician of the year."

The Belsons and the Toomeys looked genuinely interested and impressed.

Headley went on, "There's the winner—in my opinion, that is." He nodded at a busty, raven-haired young woman who had joined the Playfords on the dance floor in the company of the jeaned coin manipulator of a few minutes ago.

"I'll be damned!" murmured Belson. "A woman?"

"With a figure like that who's going to see the magic?" said Toomey with an exaggerated leer.

Dryly, his wife said, "Miss Playford, I'll warrant, for one."

Her husband chuckled and raised an eyebrow at Headley. "I don't suppose there's any chance of a couple of spare seats up the back on Sunday, old boy?"

"'Fraid not," said Headley with a smile.

"Bit of a closed shop, eh?" Belson chipped in.

"Something of the sort," replied Headley, again with a smile. "Members only and all that."

"Shame," said Toomey and sounded as if he really meant it.

They watched the four dancers, principally the physically

well-endowed magicienne, the cleavage of whose clinging red satin dress was as fine an example of precision engineering in dressmaking as one was ever likely to see.

"God knows what's keeping 'em in," muttered Toomey after a minute or two of intrigued silence. "I've often wondered what—"

"Arthur!" warned his wife. "That'll be enough, thank you. We're not at home alone in front of the television now, you know."

"Good heavens!" murmured Belson, widening his eyes. "How did that come about?" The music had ended and the two couples, Nigel Playford with the bosomy magicienne clinging possessively to his arm and gazing raptly into his face, left the floor. "Wasn't she with that other fellow?"

"It doesn't seem to matter much these days, dear," explained his wife, smiling at him condescendingly. "Not with that sort of dancing."

"Maybe not to Mr. Playford it doesn't," piped up Mrs. Toomey, "but his sister isn't too thrilled about it."

Headley, a bachelor with little experience of women's moods and how best to handle them, was thinking along the same lines; and as one of the four strong men it had taken to drag Cynthia Playford and Kath Sexton apart at Brighton, not without some justifiable alarm. There was going to be trouble of some kind over the weekend; he had sensed it the moment he had spotted Cynthia taking tea with Kath that afternoon. Cynthia was spoiling for a fight. It had been written all over her face.

"Bad-tempered–looking young woman," observed Belson, beckoning to a waiter. Everybody knew to whom he referred. "In television, is she? Some kind of actress, singer? Got that look about her."

"No," said Headley, relaxing a little as the magicienne, possibly taking the hint from the frozen stare she was getting from Cynthia, made her way back to her own table where her acne-scarred dance partner patiently awaited her in the company of an older version of the young woman herself. "Cynthia's got a rather boring job, as a matter of fact. She's a free-lance literary researcher. Authors hire her to dig up information for them on whatever subject they've decided to write a book about."

"Historical stuff, you mean?" inquired Belson, interested.

"Anything you want to know about," replied Headley. "A very broad spectrum of subjects, I believe."

"Maybe she'll do some research on you one day, Captain," said Mrs. Toomey brightly.

He shook his head and looked doubtful. "Never done anything to warrant an author taking that kind of interest in me."

"What! Not even during the war?" asked Toomey, surprised. "Surely, as a naval man, you must've had some pretty hairy scrapes in your time?"

"One or two," admitted the Captain, "but nothing that would single me out for any special attention; more's the pity."

"Maybe you should've tried just that little bit harder," joked Toomey.

"Yes," said Belson on a serious note. "I've often thought that myself."

CHAPTER 4

"That little bitch!" fumed Cynthia, stalking to the lift ahead of
her brother. She did a smart about-face. "Did you see the way
she thrust them at you when she left to go back to her table? She
nearly poked your eye out!"

"Quite an eyeful, aren't they?" he remarked, grinning.

"She's under sixteen, you know . . . fifteen last birthday,"
his sister informed him coldly. "I'm warning you, Nigel. Her
mother's just as ambitious as she is. More so."

"You mean her mother would like to go to bed with me too?"
he asked with a crooked smile.

"You know what I mean," she snapped. "Alison Crosby didn't
just happen to want to get up and dance when we did. Her
mother nudged her into it. I saw her do it, not two seconds after
we got up. And she'll nudge her into your bed before the weekend's out too."

"With a bit of luck," he murmured softly. He stepped past his
sister into the lift and she followed, watched him jab the button
for the second floor. The doors closed and the lift began its ascent.

Nigel deliberately kept his eyes trained on the moving light on
the indicator panel over the doors but was fully aware of the
venomous look that was being directed at the back of his head.
This kind of situation usually amused him: he enjoyed getting
Cynthia's back up. Tonight it merely irritated him; and worse, it
made him feel old. He sighed inaudibly. (Grow up, Cynthia;
we're neither of us kids anymore!) A smile suddenly flickered at
the corners of his mouth. Besides, all that nonsense about Alison's being under age: she was eighteen and Cynthia knew it;

and if Alison was willing (and he didn't think he'd misread the body language; he wasn't *that* old!), well, why not?

"You're asking for it, Nigel," said Cynthia sharply.

"*Mmm,*" he said, still not looking at her. "And with another bit of luck I'll get it."

They made no attempt to speak to one another again until they reached the door of Cynthia's room. As she inserted the key in the lock, she paused and turned to him. There was an odd look in her eye, an unspoken appeal.

"I mean it, you know, Nigel," she said. Her voice was very controlled, but he could sense the amount of effort it was taking her to keep it that way. "It's for your own good. I'm not being catty."

"Really?" he said indifferently. "I'll believe you, but thousands wouldn't."

"It's not—" She hesitated; shrugged. "Well, it's not as though you could really do anything for her. With her career, I mean."

"Thank you very much," he said evenly. "It's so nice to bask in the warmth of admiration of one's nearest and dearest." He considered the ill-concealed hostility in his sister's eyes and some of the old pleasure returned. Cyn had really got herself in a knot over Alison. Served her right! Maybe next time she'd think twice before throwing Henry Beamish in his face. He went on slowly, "As a matter of fact, I've already promised to help her."

Cynthia frowned. "When? You said no more than half a dozen words to her tonight."

"She came to see me at the office the other day. We had lunch together."

Cynthia stared at him. True or false? Dear God, why was it that she could never tell for sure? "Are you out of your mind? My God! What will people think?"

"That I'm a dirty old man?" he suggested.

The green eyes flashed. "Must you talk in clichés all the time? You're driving me mad: you know that, don't you?"

Nigel shrugged; gazed along the corridor. The silence between them grew longer. Then, sighing, he said, "Okay, so maybe Alison is in too much of a hurry and it wouldn't hurt her to slow down a bit, but she's got talent, Cyn. Real talent."

Cynthia glared at the Toomeys as they stepped out of the lift and came towards them. Ghastly little man! Where did he get that vulgar suit? Only a second-rate comedian would dare to wear loud checks like that! She looked back at her brother. "Yes," she said in a low, venomous hiss. "And we all know what kind of talent, don't we?" She flung open the door of her room and slammed it forcibly shut behind her.

After staring at it for a moment, her brother shrugged again and started along the corridor, keeping several paces behind the Toomeys, who seemed rather bemused by it all: Miss Playford's open hostility towards them and the scene they had just witnessed. No need to guess what that was all about!

Nigel continued to follow the couple but slowed his stride until the distance between the Toomeys and himself had lengthened considerably; then, with a faint smile, he turned abruptly on his heel, walked quickly back to the lift, and depressed the down button.

Arthur Toomey, hesitating that fraction of a second behind his wife before similarly disappearing into their room, glanced along the corridor at the man waiting for the lift and smiled knowingly to himself. A man after his own heart!

Cynthia remained standing just beyond the door, unable to move for the terrible rage which gripped her. She trembled from head to toe and clenched and unclenched her hands. Then, letting out a strangled cry, she swung herself bodily to the right and beat her forehead and fists repeatedly against the closed bathroom door. It didn't help. The voice, Henry's, in her head simply got louder and more insistent. . . . *"You're completely losing control, Cynthia; behaving like a spoilt child; don't be unreasonable—"*

She moaned and fell still, her forehead pressed up hard against the bathroom door, eyes closed. Unreasonable? She'd show them, all of them, just how unreasonable she could be!

Switching on a light, she moved weakly into the room and smoothed back her hair from her damp forehead with the palm of an equally damp hand. Then she sank unsteadily onto the foot of the bed.

Her thinking, to begin with, was confused—a jumble of crazy, illogical ideas; but gradually her mind cleared and she began to work out her plan of action.

It wasn't going to be easy. She made a fist of her right hand and nibbled at her thumbnail. She didn't know how true it was, but Nigel had once told her that the place-getters in competitions like Sunday's were customarily awarded their places as soon as the entry date had closed and the judges could come together in secret conclave and mull over the lineup of competitors. On paper, that is. Only very rarely (this was according to Nigel) would an amateur be awarded a place over a professional, those rare occasions when an amateur was placed first, second, or third as often as not being determined by the mood of the audience and the willingness of the judges to fly in the face of their hostility if they made a bad award. In those instances, where an amateur turned in a far superior performance to the professional, Nigel said the judges generally capitulated and played it safe, awarded a joint first prize or a joint second as the case may be. That way everybody was happy: the audience was appeased, the amateur delighted, and no harm done to the professional's prestige!

Cynthia gnawed anxiously at her thumbnail. It all sounded logical and reasonable enough—the professional entertainer being protected in this way—but she wasn't sure: that sort of thing was Nigel all over, making an accusation like this and then backing it up with a logical argument and it all being absolute nonsense, his way of needling her over Frank Sexton, who was usually the first to be invited to sit on the panel of judges for these competitions.

The weakened thumbnail finally split and Cynthia examined the damage, frowning. Nobody had approached her about Sunday, so assuming that she wasn't deliberately being left out in the cold by the other three judges (Nigel, Frank, and Lance Headley), then the competition wasn't fixed. (Or if it were, then she wasn't going to be told about it, which wouldn't altogether surprise her.) Though there was still time, all day tomorrow. . . .

The broken thumbnail went back into her mouth, and she stripped a sliver from it with her teeth. Somewhere at the back of her mind she seemed to remember Nigel bemoaning the fact that no professionals had bothered to enter the competition. Or was it the other way round—some had, but none of them amounted to much? No, she was pretty sure she had got it right the first time; there were no professionals in the competition. One or two aspirants, possibly, but no one whose sole means of earning a living could be jeopardised by his or her failure to be placed in a competition of this kind, with all its attendant publicity in the magic media. (This was supposing that Nigel hadn't been making the lot of it up as he went along, purely to bait her over Frank!) Alison Crosby was therefore in with a chance, a *good* chance, thought Cynthia, who hadn't actually seen the young magicienne on stage but had heard enough about her from others to know that what Nigel had said was true. She was good. Lance Headley thought so too: he'd made no secret of it, was openly biased in the girl's favour. So that made it two votes for Alison (Nigel's and Lance's) and one against (hers). Three to one if Frank also liked the girl.

Cynthia's eyes narrowed. Frank's opinion of Alison would undoubtedly have considerable sway—with Lance Headley, who always kept an eye to the main chance (*yes, Your Magnificence; no, Your Magnificence; may I kiss your feet, Your Magnificence?*), if not with Nigel. And that, she smiled thinly, put an entirely different complexion on matters. Three to one *against* . . . if Frank could be persuaded not to vote for the girl. A possibility, anyway. Frank could be infuriatingly chauvinistic at times; and he was well known not to care too much for magiciennes, regardless of how talented they were. But if the audience liked Alison on Sunday, and she turned in a good performance . . .

Cynthia sighed. Back to square one. She blew softly on her broken thumbnail, drying it. Perhaps not quite back where she had started. She did have one ace up her sleeve; and she'd use it too if Frank forced her hand. Not that he would have any illusions about whether or not she was bluffing. He had seen her too often in action, even joked about it, said he hoped he'd be around the day she finally came unstuck—

Cynthia's hands flew to her ears, covering them, blocking out Henry's gently persuasive voice urging her not to be unreasonable, but to be realistic. Gasping a little, she stumbled to her feet and groped her way to the telephone, very nearly dragging it onto the floor as she snatched up the receiver.

She waited. The seconds ticked silently and unproductively by; her free hand clenched and unclenched; she started to curse.

The hotel operator, accustomed to such ill-mannered behaviour, or with a thicker skin than most, endured the stream of abuse which assailed her eventual response by simply waiting in silence and letting the "nut case" in Room 23 get the venom out of her system.

"Please arrange," demanded Cynthia at length, very breathlessly (she was trembling all over again), "for someone to call Mr. Frank Sexton to the phone immediately, please. He can be located in the Wellington Room."

"To speak to you, Madam?" inquired the girl at the other end, politely.

"No," said Cynthia, her voice smooth as silk. "To the President of the United States." She changed hands and dried the palm of her sweaty right hand, the one formerly holding the receiver, down the side of her grey, floor-length woollen skirt. "Just tell Mr. Sexton that he's wanted urgently on the phone." She hesitated. "No, don't say that. . . ." She smiled into the mouthpiece and her eyes glittered maliciously. "Tell him, please, that Cynthia Playford—you've got that, *Cynthia* Playford?— wants to talk to him right away. It's urgent—"

CHAPTER 5

The graveyard had not been used since early this century: September 1902 was the last time; and nowadays the only creatures who visited this solitary place were the handful of bedraggled sheep which occasionally strayed there from nearby farms, and a few shaggy-coated goats. That was until Cynthia Playford, spinster, of Broadstairs in Kent, at approximately seven minutes past the hour of ten on Easter Saturday morning, plummeted out of the skies.

There were only five witnesses to her death dive into the graveyard; three sheep, a black-faced newborn lamb, and one thoroughly depraved-looking billy goat. The sheep hardly noticed the stranger in their midst: only one of their number, the ewe with the lamb, lifted its head from its grazing to contemplate the lifeless body—at first glance little more than a bundle of clothing—impaled on the high, rusted spiked railing surrounding the Anstey family plot, and the goat which nibbled at the long slash of bright red that was a scarf.

The expression on the ewe's face was inscrutable: this sort of thing might have been a daily occurrence; human beings regularly fell out of the sky onto the spiked railing enclosing the Anstey plot to provide some dietary relief for its friends, the goats. (The one eating the woollen scarf was making an absolute pig of itself!)

Something like an hour later, after years of having the place almost entirely to themselves, more human beings had arrived: these the more conventional way on foot, scrambling, sometimes —when they would lose their balance—on all fours, along the narrow ridges made in the rock-strewn, sparsely vegetated hillside by the cloven-hooved animals. The narrow unmade carriageway which in Victorian times had served as an access road to the graveyard had disappeared under a landslide fifty years ago.

The billy goat was having its dessert by this time, a lady's fashionable medium-heeled shoe which it had found lying about somewhere or other on the bleak hillside. The humans were none too pleased about this, and a chase, of sorts, ensued—the outcome of which was predictable from the outset. The nimble-footed goat was last seen disappearing into the next valley, still in possession of its half-finished second course, leaving in its wake one twisted ankle, a ruined bobby's helmet, an assortment of cuts and bruises, and some foul, language-polluted air.

At nine o'clock the following morning, Easter Sunday, despite intermittent sunshine, it was a grey, dismal place; desolate. Unfriendly, thought ex–Detective Chief Superintendent David Sayer as he stood with Detective Chief Inspector Griffith Walsh of the local CID before the Anstey family plot and surveyed the valley. There was a biting wind, and the two men had turned up the collars on their coats and kept their backs to it as much as they could.

The Chief Inspector was fifty-two years old, Welsh, of medium height and build, and dark, a heavy shadow already shading in the lower portion of his face even though it was less than two hours since he had risen from his bed and shaved. He was a dour-looking man with occasional matching flashes of wit and had changed little, thought Sayer, since he and Walsh were young recruits at police college together where they had become close friends, remaining so until their respective careers ultimately intervened and took them their separate ways.

Walsh also had a streaming head cold and blew his nose almost constantly into one or the other of two handkerchiefs which he had prudently brought along with him.

"Not really geared for this kind of investigation," he commented, wiping his nose vigorously and then fingering it tentatively. It was red and looked very sore. "Especially over a holiday weekend with the town bursting at the seams with tourists. It would've been different if it had been one of our own, somebody local; but with people coming and going all the time, visitors from all four corners of the British Isles, some from even as far afield as the Continent and America, well–" he shrugged "–you know how it is; and I've an idea we'll find our answer to this one back in the Home Counties, anyway." Walsh's voice didn't match his physical appearance: it was slow and quiet and had the gentle musical lilt to it indigenous to those parts.

Sayer nodded noncommittally and gazed up at the thick black cables which lined the cloud-patched sky. Tall, metal-laced pylons (four were visible to the two men from their vantage point in the graveyard) reached in a sweeping arc skywards from one side of the valley to the other and into the valley beyond (Walsh had already pointed out to Sayer), right to the summit of Great Mountain. The cable between the evenly spaced pylons, one of which was to the immediate right of the two men, was slack so that a cabin, as it approached each pylon, went into a slightly more pronounced climb until, with a jolt and a sickening lurch, it was through the junction and on its way to the next pylon on its steady climb up the mountain.

In Sayer's opinion—one he had voiced some years earlier when inspecting the tourist attraction at the behest of the insurance company which provided the operator with a personal liability cover—*cabin* lift was a misnomer. The "cabins" were not fully enclosed as one would have imagined, but more like four-seater buckets.

"It's a weird feeling going through those junctions," Walsh remarked, more to himself than to the man with him. "Particularly that one back there near the ridge–" He was pointing ahead of them at a pylon some way off in the distance with a jutting, plateau-topped ridge for a backdrop. "You're convinced that your cabin's going to jump the cable; and while you're worrying about that–" he looked at Sayer "–I'm talking now about the ascent, when you're approaching the ridge from the starting-out point beyond it (you can't see the landing stage from here,

but it's just past the ridge), you're through the junction and
your eyes are immediately drawn down here into this valley
straight on to the graveyard; and believe me, with something
like another dozen of those junctions up ahead of you, it's not a
heartening sight. My kids loved the thing when I took them up
for a ride on it for the first time; but let me tell you this, once
was enough for me. It certainly wasn't my idea of having a nice
time. I was glad to get out of the damn thing. Completely safe,
of course: it just doesn't seem like it. Yesterday's 'accident' was
the first fatality that's occurred in the ten years the cabin lift has
been in operation. There have been minor injuries, naturally—
youngsters getting their fingers shut in the cabin gate, that sort
of thing—but never anything major until now."

Reluctantly, Walsh turned his back on the ridge and faced
into the wind and pointed along the valley at the dark mountain
glowering in the far distance. "There's a cable car up there at
the top, something like an old-fashioned tram car which, if you
wish, you can take to the foot of the other side of the mountain
in preference to making the return trip by the cabin lift; and I'm
not kidding you, I was the first one on it. Good old terra firma for
me every time."

A red cabin, creeping like some giant bug across the sky, was
approaching them now; the two men watched it pass overhead.
As it receded into the distance they could see its three match-
stick occupants, just their heads and shoulders.

"Listen to that sound it makes as it goes through the junction,
will you?" said Walsh with the depth of feeling born of a well-
remembered, thoroughly unpleasant experience. He put his
handkerchief to his nose and used it robustly, which might or
might not have been a deliberate expression of his own personal
sentiments concerning Plaid-yro-Wyth's principal tourist attraction. Then, thrusting his hands into his pockets: "The way I see
it, the dead woman wasn't pushed, she didn't jump or accidentally fall, she was thrown or tipped overboard. There's not much
of her—you'll see that for yourself; that's if you're interested and

want to take a look at her. Any man of average height and build could lift her, I'd say, without too much trouble."

Walsh drew out his handkerchief again and made ready to use it. "I don't know how familiar you are with the whole setup and its general operation, but there's a gate on the left-hand side of each cabin which is secured on the outside by an attendant before it sets off up the mountain. The gate is then opened at the other end by another attendant and the passengers let out. I might be wrong, but I personally don't think that anyone in his right mind would risk touching the gate once the cabin got under way. For obvious reasons, the design of the cabins is such that it's difficult to get at the gate catch from the inside—though I must admit I haven't tried, I'm taking Hugh Owens' (that's the owner of the cabin lift) and the attendant's word for it there; but if some idiot was messing about with the catch and the gate fell open too quickly—" he fumbled for the handkerchief which only seconds before he had returned to his coat pocket "—or unexpectedly, say, at a junction where the cabin gives this terrible jolting lurch forward—"

Walsh shook his head dolefully and used the handkerchief, then put it away. "I can't really see it myself. Still, stranger things, as they say . . . where there's a will, there's always a way. There were no marks on the deceased's body other than the three deep wounds in her chest where the iron spikes—" he indicated his head at the spiked railing round the grave in front of which they were standing "—went in, and some scratches and a deep cut on her right hand, again from the spikes; so it would seem unlikely that a struggle took place up there preceding her fall."

Walsh didn't sound too convinced about it and confirmed his doubtfulness over this particular theory by confessing, "I've an idea she might've been unconscious, knocked senseless first before being tossed out—it's the only way I can honestly see it happening: but then that—" he shrugged "—as I've said, doesn't tie in with what Doc Hughes, the medical examiner, had to tell us. There was definitely no bruising or marking to the face or head."

He looked at Sayer wonderingly. "But surely she didn't willingly let herself be picked up and heaved out?"

Sayer said, "No possibility she could've jumped of her own free will?"

"A suicide?" Walsh sounded even more doubtful. "She could have, I suppose—but only with considerable difficulty. And why pay to go up there to do it? There are plenty of other places here in the mountains she could've picked to leap from, and for free. And again, with suicide there'd almost certainly have been marks on her body . . . bruising, scratches on both hands and her legs (torn tights, perhaps); and you'd need to be fairly athletic, you know. You couldn't, for example, lean too far and fall out. You'd have to be quite deliberate about it—clamber up onto the seat, then climb over the side, one leg at a time; or if you wanted to be really spectacular about it, get onto the seat and then sit on the side of the cabin and let yourself fall over backwards—like a scuba diver. I daresay there are any number of ways you could do it if you'd a mind to, but it wouldn't be easy. And what about this big burly bloke the two witnesses have said was sitting in the cabin with her: what's he doing all this time . . . while she's getting herself into position ready for the big jump? He's not taking a nap, I can tell you that! The moment anybody started moving around in one of those things, you'd be sitting up taking notice and doing something positive about it, like telling them to sit still, for Christ's sake, and stop rocking the boat! You take a ride in one of the things and you'll know exactly what I mean. Half the time you're too scared to breathe!"

Sayer asked, "Who spotted the body?"

"One of the women who work in the café up at the summit. She took the cabin lift to work as usual at ten-twenty or thereabouts. The café opens at eleven. When she got to the top, she mentioned to the attendant up there that she'd seen something in the graveyard—you couldn't be really sure from up there what it was . . . it could've been some old clothing, or even a guy somebody—youngsters—had made and carted down here from the road for a bit of a lark; you know, to scare hell out of the passengers in the cabin lift as they came over the ridge and went through the first junction. That happened once before. Anyway, it had to be checked out, just in case. Owens, the cabin-lift proprietor, phoned us and reported the matter, and a couple of our chaps came down and took a closer look."

Sayer nodded, and with a backwards glance at the Anstey grave and its hideous iron railing, he started back the way they had come, through the graveyard past the lichen-covered angel with sorrowing eyes and arms cast heavenwards, and then along the animal trails which laced the hillside.

Walsh, following a few steps behind him, said, "There are only the two witnesses that we've been able to trace who saw the woman and the man together. The ticket seller at the cabin lift and Will Llewellyn. Will's a mechanic; works for Owens too."

Walsh paused and blew his nose quietly. "No apprenticeship ticket, or anything like that. Will's not quite all there, poor devil. But there's nothing he doesn't know, or can't teach himself, about machinery." Walsh was beginning to pant with the exertion of combining a reasonably difficult climb over very rough, uneven ground with conversation and his heavy cold. "Virtually keeps that cabin lift running single-handed for Owens.

"Will's usually the first there in the morning: it's his job to do the trial run, a safety precaution. He sends the first cabin of the day—empty, of course—up to the top of the mountain, and somebody there turns it round and sends it back down again. No member of the public is allowed to use the cabin lift until the test run has been done first thing each morning. This is at approximately nine-fifteen. It takes about forty to forty-five minutes for the test-run cabin to go up and come back down again. Then at ten o'clock the attendant opens up the turnstile and the public is allowed through. The cabin the deceased and the man got into was the second up the mountain yesterday morning—the one immediately after the test run had been completed."

Sayer, himself beginning to pant with exertion, said, "What about the cabin attendant? Didn't he see the woman and the man?"

"No, he didn't turn up for work yesterday; Will took his place. Will got the better look at them. The chap in the ticket box only saw them fleetingly, when he took their money for the ride and again when they were about to get in the cabin."

"They paid their fares separately?" panted Sayer.

Walsh, who was using his handkerchief again, said a muffled, "Yes, that's right. The woman first, then the man. A minute or two apart. The ticket seller couldn't say if they knew one another; and Will . . . well, it's pretty hopeless asking Will that kind of question; he wouldn't know what you were talking about. Two people standing together are two people standing together; the finer complexities of whether or not they knew each other and were friends would be beyond his mental capacity."

They paused to catch their breath.

"Will shut the gate after the two of them had got into the cabin?" asked Sayer.

"I know what you're thinking," puffed Walsh, nodding. He took a deep breath. "Will being ten pence short in the pound; and you're not the first to wonder about it." He shrugged and made a face. "It's possible, I suppose, that Will was careless and didn't secure the gate properly after them: that's a mistake even the regular attendant (anybody) could make; but I can't really see Will making that kind of slip. It's as simple and natural as breathing to Will—anything mechanical: fitting one part into another, locking things up. I've often wondered what a psychologist would make of him. Put anything mechanical in front of him, all in bits and pieces, and make it as complicated as you like, and Will'll have it together and working in next to no time. But as for his general IQ—"

He shook his head and they moved on, Walsh swearing as he lost his footing and slithered several feet in slimy mud onto his hands and trousered knees. He had a struggle to get back onto his feet, which kept slithering out from under him; but he got there eventually, cursing irritably as he brushed ineffectually with his hands at the muddy streaks on his black topcoat and trousers.

Sayer was in similar difficulties, though so far only his leather-gloved hands and shoes had got dirtied. He paused for a moment and gazed back down the valley to the graveyard. He didn't really think the insurers had anything to worry about—other than his fee for their ruining his holiday weekend!

CHAPTER 6

It took them an exhausting twenty minutes to climb back up to the road and the unmarked police car which was parked there waiting for them. A ten-minute drive, keeping to the tortuous bitumenised road chiselled out of the mountainside, brought them down from the valley to the entrance to the cabin lift.

The owner, Hugh Owens, who was expecting Walsh and the insurance investigator and had seen their car approaching, was waiting for them outside the turnstile where business was extremely brisk. A restless queue of adults and children trailed back down the gently curving road and disappeared out of sight. Those waiting at the tail end of the queue would have an hour or more's wait before they would get their turn for a ride up the mountain.

Owens took Walsh and Sayer straight through to his small, unheated one-room office behind the ticket box and motioned them into two of the three vacant chairs which he had set out ready for them. He himself perched on a corner of his dusty, paper-cluttered desk.

He was short, ruddy-jowled, in his late middle age, and like Walsh, inclined to be dour of expression. His speaking voice was even more singsongy than the Chief Inspector's, but had a slightly rougher edge to it.

"Can't say this has been a bad thing for business," he remarked as the other two men sat down. "The take's already twice up on what it was at this time last Easter Sunday. More turning up all the time. Nothing for them to see, of course. I guess it's just the morbid thrill of knowing what happened up there yesterday: they want to go through the harrowing experience for themselves . . . imagine what it would be like to fall that way. Funny people, humans."

He rubbed his hands briskly together, possibly in anticipation of the money he would take that day, but probably to warm them. The room was cold and damp, musty-smelling, but he made no move to switch on the dusty, ancient-looking electric fire which continued to stand in a corner of the room getting no younger and gathering even more dust.

Owens' gaze rested momentarily on Walsh, then moved on to Sayer. "Well, gentlemen, how can I help you?" He answered his question himself. "Not as much as I'd like to be able to, I'm afraid. I wasn't here, you know: I seldom come in on Saturdays much before midday. Nell—that's the wife—likes me to take her shopping . . . to help her carry the bags. Luckily, we hadn't left home yesterday morning when young Davey, the lad who usually looks after things up at the other end—" he explained to Sayer "—phoned to report that there was something in the graveyard (just another Guy Fawkes dummy, he thought) and asked me what I wanted done about it. Avoids any hysteria, you see: you get a good view of the graveyard from up there in the cabins, and we don't want people's imaginations running away with them, do we?

"The graveyard puts a lot of people off a return trip by the cabin lift, and—" Owens came close to a smile "—I don't own the cable car up at the summit, the alternative means of getting down the mountain . . . other than for Shanks' pony, of course. The cable car's owned and operated by the Town Council in direct competition with me, so the graveyard's good business for them; but—" another near smile "—that doesn't mean I have to help them take the bread out of my mouth by letting the kids get away with littering up the graveyard with their dummy dead bodies—their idea of a joke, you see. Still, that's not why you gentlemen are here, is it, to listen to me go on about my problems? Now, you're going to want to talk to my staff—"

Sayer said, "Could I have a word first with the young man—

Will Llewellyn—who put the man and the woman into the cabin yesterday?"

Owens nodded, stepped down from his perch, and went to a sliding, pebble-glassed panel in the wall behind his visitors. Drawing it aside, he said to the ticket seller, whose back and shoulders only were visible, "Give Will a shout for me, will you, Eli?" Then he closed the panel and returned to his desk, this time sitting up to it in a chair.

"Will's a good lad," he said. "But you know how it is; a small place like this where pretty well everybody knows everybody else always has its resident simpleton, and ours is Will. In his own way, I guess you could say he's quite a celebrity. Oh, and incidentally—"

There was a soft tap, just one, on the door; and Owens broke off and sang out, "In you come, lad."

A tall, dark, good-looking young man of about twenty wearing black, grease-stiffened overalls entered the room. His lack of IQ was not immediately apparent from his general appearance; it was something, more a suspicion over some of his movements which were not quite co-ordinated, that grew as time progressed. His speech was a little slower than normal; and he considered the questions put to him for a very long time, even for the most cautious of people, before answering them.

Owens introduced him to the insurance investigator. Walsh, of course, he already knew.

Owens continued, "Sit yourself down, lad." He waved Will into the vacant chair. "No need to stand on ceremony. Mr. Sayer would like to have a word with you about the lady who had the accident yesterday morning."

Will thought about it, wriggling his buttocks until the base of his spine came up hard against the back of the chair. He showed no concern at being summoned to the guv'nor's office to speak to the insurance investigator, only a mild interest. "The one what fell?" he asked Owens.

"That's right, Will," said Owens. "You remember her, don't you? You said she was pretty."

Will stared at him and nodded.

Sayer, smiling at the young man, said, "Tell me about her, Will. Did she speak to you?"

Will shook his head.

"What about when she got into the cabin, Will, and gave you her ticket?" asked Owens, anxious to help. "Didn't she say something to you then?"

"Nuthin'," he said. "She never said nuthin'."

"Did she smile at you?" ventured Sayer.

"Nuthin'," the young man reiterated. "Just gave me a bad look."

"Angry," Owens explained quickly. "That means she was angry."

Sayer said kindly, "Was the lady angry with you, Will?"

He considered the suggestion. "I never done nuthin' to her. Just took her ticket. Then the man's."

Sayer said, "Was the lady angry with the man, do you think?"

Will gave him a blank stare. "Dunno. She never said nuthin' to me."

"Did she say anything to the man?" persisted Sayer.

"Nuthin'," the young man repeated. "She never said nuthin' to no one. Just sat there and looked bad."

Sayer changed tack. "What about the man then? Did he speak to you?"

Will frowned at him.

Owens interceded. "What about saying 'thank you,' Will?"

Will stared at Owens for a moment; then, puzzled, he looked at Sayer and thanked him politely.

"No, you daft thing," said Owens good-naturedly. "I don't mean you. The man yesterday. Did he say 'thank you' when you took his ticket and put him in the cabin?"

Will shook his head. "He was a nice man. He never gave me a bad look. He smiled."

Sayer said, "Where did they sit, Will, after they got into the cabin? Side by side—next to each other?"

Will shook his head and frowned.

Sayer gave him an encouraging smile. "The lady sat on one side and the man on the other, facing her? Like that, Will?"

The young man smiled back and nodded contentedly.

Owens interrupted. He seemed anxious to speed things up a little, this part of the interrogation, anyway, and possibly because he was unsure and fearful of the consequences to himself and his insurance policy should negligence on the part of any of his employees be proven. "The man faced the way they were travelling, Will said."

Sayer nodded. "What did this man look like, Will?"

Will frowned and shook his head perplexedly.

"Was he a young man, Will?" asked Sayer patiently. "Old?"

Silence. A long, unwavering stare.

"Was his hair grey?" asked Sayer. "Or very dark like Mr. Walsh's?"

The young man made a thoughtful appraisal of the last remaining strands of long black hair carefully combed across Walsh's scalp. "Like the guv'nor's," said Will flatly.

As one, Sayer and Walsh looked at the cabin-lift proprietor and noted that he had a reasonable head of hair for a man of his years, the bulk of which was brownish black with wide wings of uninterrupted grey at the sides near his temples.

Walsh said, "What about the scarf, Will? Remember the long woollen one you said the man had round his head and face to keep out the cold?" Walsh looked at Sayer and shrugged. "Will made no reference to the man's hair yesterday when we took a statement from him. He told us then that it was covered up with a woollen scarf."

The young man seemed unsure; he looked at Owens, then at Walsh, and finally at Sayer, who said, "Never mind, Will. Let's talk about something else—the man's clothes. Can you remember what he was wearing?"

Will looked at his employer.

"Go on, lad," Owens urged him. "You remember the coat you told me and Mr. Walsh about yesterday. You tell Mr. Sayer—"

Will shifted his gaze to the insurance investigator.

Walsh said coaxingly, "Come along, Will; there's a good lad. Tell Mr. Sayer about the pretty lining. You remember that, don't you? You remembered it all right yesterday."

No reaction.

Walsh gave him another few moments; then, shrugging resignedly, he said, "Some kind of raincoat, grey or fawn . . . Will's not too good on colours—I don't know if it's due to colour blindness or because he never learnt them to begin with; but the important thing is that the coat was lined with some kind of plaid—a red tartan—material. I think, from the description we managed to get from Will yesterday, it could be something like the mac Harold Wilson made famous when he was Prime Minister."

Sayer nodded and smiled at the young man. "That's fine, Will. You've been a big help." He looked at Owens. "I think that'll be all I need Will for for the moment, thank you. If I could just have a few words now with your ticket seller?"

Owens rose and gestured to Will. "Right, lad. Off you go." He followed the young man out of the office; and a minute or so later, Elias Jones, the ticket seller, came in alone. Owens had taken his place in the window at the turnstile.

CHAPTER 7

Walsh did the introductions; he told Eli to be seated, that this wouldn't take long.

"Now, Mr. Jones," said Sayer. "I understand that you sold tickets to the woman who was killed yesterday and to the man who went up on the cabin lift with her."

Elias Jones, rake-thin, dark, with sagging sepia-tinted bags under his eyes, a long chin and prominent nose, and even less hair on top of his head than Walsh had, nodded. "Can't say I remember them all that well, except to say that they was the first —our first customers for the day."

Eli covered his mouth momentarily with his right hand. He had some kind of upper dental plate which kept riding up and down quite independently of his own teeth as he spoke.

Dental problems sorted out, Eli went on, "After them two, nobody came along . . . *oooh*—" he pursed his thin lips, squinted "—I'd say for the best part of ten, fifteen minutes, maybe more. Ethel was next, after them—one of the women what works up at the caf'. Slow it was yesterday. Early morning, that is. Picked up later on in the day. Saturday morning's always slow; but that's when most folks gets their chores done . . . the shopping, go down to the laundrette. Eleven, eleven-thirty—that's when they start rolling up. Go up the caf' for a bite to eat for their lunch; then they have themselves a ride back down again on the cable car. Some even walk—" The tone of his voice expressed some surprise about this. "Takes a while, mind. Murder on the back of the legs!"

Sayer said, "You say you don't remember the man and the woman too well?"

Eli tweaked the tip of his hooked nose from side to side between a greasy, money-soiled thumb and forefinger. "Her . . . maybe I remember her, just a bit. But that was because she was here first and had to hang about while Will finished the test run. Nice-looking woman: not really what you'd call pretty, but you noticed her all right, if you follow my meaning."

Sayer nodded. "Did she speak to you at all?"

"Just said the usual thing," replied the ticket seller, shrugging, "how much was the fare— There it was, plain as the nose on your face, for all to see—" he breathed wearily "—but they all ask the same question . . . the women do, anyway. Men are more observant, not so lazy—" He grinned. "I told her she'd have to wait a bit, we wasn't open yet; and then before she could give me an argument (that's another thing you've got to put up with, people what won't take no for an answer!), I explained that we was still doing the test run and that I'd be breaking the law and lose my job if I sold anybody a ticket for a ride before I'd been given the all clear. Ten o'clock, that was when we'd be open, I said, and she'd have to come back then."

"What time was this?" asked Sayer.

" 'Bout ten to, I think. She looked at her watch—" Eli screwed up his eyes and tried to remember what had happened next "—I think she said something about it being fast, it was already ten by her . . . past ten, in fact, I think she said. Then she wandered off. Ten minutes later—Will was just about to unlock the turnstile —she came back and bought her ticket (a single) and went on through to the landing stage. Then the man came up and bought his ticket and he went on through."

Sayer said, "Did he ask for a single or a return?"

"He never spoke," said Eli. "He had the right money ready for a single, which is what most folk want, so that was what I gave him."

"Where was he standing in relation to the woman once they went through to the landing stage?" asked Sayer.

"A bit behind her," replied Eli. "Like he was being a gentleman and letting her go first. I didn't take no notice of them after that. There was a cabin there ready and waiting to go; and when I looked out a couple of minutes later they'd both gone, shared the same cabin. They don't have to if they'd rather not . . . only if we're very busy; then we've got to keep things moving and fill all the cabins whether folk like it or not. Joe—that's the regular attendant who didn't show up for work yesterday—would've asked them, seeing as they was strangers and it was quiet, whether they minded sharing; but Will—" Eli's hand shot up to his mouth as the dental plate almost catapulted out of it "—well, them sort of refinements wouldn't occur to poor Will, now would they? He'd just open up the gate, wait for whoever was there to climb aboard—four's the most we let in at a time—then he'd shut it up and off it'd go with them; they could like it or lump it."

Sayer asked, "Who operates the cabin lift?"

"Out in the control room, you mean? Will, of course." The ticket seller was quite taken aback by Sayer's ignorance. Everyone in the whole wide world, apparently, knew that about Will: everyone, that is, except the pudding head from the insurance company. "It's Will's job to work them big levers out the back of the landing stage. Nobody would dare touch them while Will's about the place," he said emphatically. "The guv'nor, of course: Will don't mind him touching them. But if Joe or me dared, or any of the others—" Eli's lips pursed and he sucked in air. "Got a temper has Will, 'bout some things, them levers in partic'lar."

Sayer nodded thoughtfully. "I see— So after Will secured the gate on the cabin, he had to go back to the control room and operate the mechanism that lifts the cabins up and down the mountain?"

Eli frowned. "Well, I don't know about that, what he did yesterday. I mean, as far as I know, once he puts them levers in gear (or whatever it is he does with them) and everything gets rolling, that's it; he just has to keep an eye on things . . . seems to spend a heck of a lot of time just wandering about back there with an oily rag in his hand, wiping this and polishing that, and not doing much of anything else that I've ever been able to make out. I didn't see exactly what he did yesterday; I wasn't watching. Maybe he had to leave the cabin for a moment while he went into the control room and worked them levers; and then again, maybe not. If everything was all set ready to go, then all he would've had to do (this was once he'd got the man and the woman settled down in the cabin) would be to drag it forward for a couple of yards—that's the job Joe usually does—and then give it a little swing out so it was clear of the landing stage; and that would've been it, away it would've gone up the mountain."

"Will did that all day on his own, as well as keeping an eye on things in the control room?" asked Sayer.

"You've gotta be joking!" said Eli, and gave the pudding head a pitying look. "You couldn't run things that way for long. What if something went wrong with the machinery? Will couldn't be in two places at once, could he now? We had somebody—a replacement for Joe—here by the time the next customer rolled up wanting to buy a ticket."

"Coming back to the woman and the man," said Sayer. "It wasn't your impression that they knew one another?"

"That's the way it looked to me," said Eli, nodding. "I'd say they was complete strangers, though I wasn't paying that much attention to them, mind." He paused and thought for a moment. "It's possible, I suppose, that they'd had a bit of a tiff and weren't speaking to each other. She looked a bad-tempered one, the sort who'd argue just for the sake of it. Then again, who knows . . . maybe it was one of them clandestine meetings and they was making sure nobody was around to hear what they was talking about."

Sayer said, "Will told us the woman—"

"Gave him a bad look?" finished Eli, widening his eyes. "Says that about most folk." He smiled patronizingly at Sayer. "He'll probably tell me tomorrow that *you* gave him a bad look!"

Sayer nodded. "Can you describe the man?"

Eli considered the question. "No— I never looked at his face, just his hand when he pushed the money across the counter for his ticket; then when I looked up a couple of minutes later, he was standing on the landing stage with his back to me . . . well, sort of side on. I couldn't really see all that much of them, anyway: the sun came out at that moment and they was in shadow—the landing stage being under cover, you see. I can only tell you that he was tall and that he was wearing a raincoat. I'm not even sure what colour it was, grey or fawn. One or t'other."

"Was he wearing gloves?" asked Sayer, and Walsh smiled to himself. Insurance investigator? Like hell he was. Once a copper always a copper!

Eli said, "No. Nice hand it was. I see all kinds, I do; but that was a real nice one. Nice clean nails."

"Any rings or distinguishing marks? Moles?" suggested Sayer. "Half-moons on the fingernails, perhaps?"

Eli shook his head slowly. "No. It was just a real nice hand, the kind a man'd be proud to have, a proper gentleman's hand . . . somebody who'd never done a day's dirty work in his life. But don't get me wrong there; that hand didn't belong to no sissy—" the long bony finger Eli directed at Sayer emphasized the point "—I can tell you that much. He'd be the—" Eli covered his mouth quickly and deftly tongued his dental plate back into place "—sort of person who'd be used to power, in a high position . . . y'know, the guv'nor, good at giving orders (been given orders himself in his time, knows how to take them too): someone who's been around; knows how to handle himself in a tricky situation."

Eli smiled smugly. "You can tell a lot about a person by looking at his hands; and I'm not talking about palmistry, neither. That rubbish! Says a lot about a person if they take good care of their hands. Most people don't, you see. They splash it all about, the aftershave—never give their hands and fingernails a second thought. Terrible specimens I get to see with this job. Of course—" Eli gave the insurance investigator another patronising smile, began to relax and enjoy himself, crossing his legs to make himself more comfortable, then almost immediately uncrossing them and sitting up to attention with an abrupt "Oh!" His face fell. "That's all, is it?"

Sayer was getting slowly to his feet. Walsh quickly followed suit. Eli was the last to rise, the least anxious to stir himself and be on about his business.

"You've been very helpful, Mr. Jones," said Sayer. "Thank you. I won't detain you from your work any longer."

"I'll be getting back then," said Eli. He hesitated, seemed even more dissatisfied that the interview was at an end.

Sayer glanced at him, recognised the signs, and knew he would probably regret this but decided to risk it. "Yes, Mr. Jones?" he said. "You've thought of something else?"

"No," Eli admitted. "Not really. It's just that . . . well, I might as well get it off my chest: I won't be satisfied until I do—" His gaze ranged hopefully over Walsh and the insurance investigator as he gave each his turn to offer up some sign or word of encouragement for him to continue. It was the Chief Inspector who responded.

"Spit it out, Eli," he said curtly. "We've not got all day."

Eli looked hurt. He shrugged. "It didn't surprise me: that was all I was going to say."

Sayer said mildly, "What didn't surprise you, Mr. Jones?"

"Oh, you know," he said, piqued. Serve them bleeding right if they never caught the fellow; see if he cared! He shrugged indifferently. "That he turned out to be a killer. I—" He hesitated, looked from Walsh to Sayer and then finally back at Walsh, to whom he nodded sagely. "That bloke's killed before; that's what I think. I've got that hand imprinted on my mind; and that's what I see . . . a man who can give orders, a man who can take them and not ask questions. *A professional killer.*"

Walsh said dourly, *"Mmm,* and we're really British agents hunting down Russian spies; and you'll probably get an O.B.E. for your services to the nation today." The Chief Inspector waved him aside impatiently. "Too much television, Eli. I'd—"

Sayer restrained Walsh with a slight movement of his head; and Eli, glimpsing the gesture out of the corner of his eye, looked round at him expectantly.

"Go on, Mr. Jones," said Sayer pleasantly. "You were saying—?"

Eli flashed Walsh a defiant look and said, "I think he was a hired killer—some kind of paid assassin, that's what he was. The kind of man the Mafia uses . . . you know, a 'hit' man. Somebody hired him to kill that woman, to follow her up here and get in that cabin with her."

"An interesting theory, Mr. Jones," said Sayer, moving ahead of him towards the door. "I'm sure Mr. Walsh will bear it in mind."

CHAPTER 8

Walsh shook his head. "Hired assassin! If you ask me, Eli's been cooped up too long in that ticket box; it's time they pensioned him off."

He unlocked the door of the police car, got in, and started it up. "Well—" he wound down the window; looked up at Sayer "—remember what I said. Anything I can do to help . . . I'll be at The Grand somewhere around noon. Drop in, if you've a moment, and have a bite to eat and a chat."

The car moved off and Sayer turned back to the cabin-lift proprietor, who was waiting for him on the far side of the turnstile. Waving Sayer through ahead of everyone else, Owens then gestured to the ticket seller and said, "Hold up everything here for a few minutes, will you, Eli?"

Owens, leading the way, stepped up onto the landing stage and indicated to Sayer where the insurance investigator ought to stand so as not to be in the way while the half-dozen or so people already waiting there were despatched on their way up the mountain by the attendant.

Sayer could see Will through one of the two picture windows in the control room which overlooked the landing stage. He was standing at close attention by his brightly polished levers and didn't once look the insurance investigator's way.

"The police don't know for sure which cabin the woman and the man went up in," said Owens while they waited for the attendant to become free. Owens was apparently bothered by silences and seemed to consider himself under some obligation to do something about the one which had suddenly descended upon them. Then he became concerned that he might have spoken out of turn. "They were very thorough, though . . . went over every single one of them, left no stone unturned," he assured Sayer. "But under the circumstances—" He extended an arm and widened his eyes. "Well, you can see for yourself; they all look alike, don't they? And it wasn't as though it was a messy murder, was it? I mean—" he frowned as if again afraid he might have spoken out of turn "—that's if it was murder."

Sayer pictured Cynthia Playford impaled on the spiked iron railings and wondered just how much messier Owens would have liked it; though he realised, of course, what the man had really meant. The killer, assuming there was one, had only acted out his intent to commit murder in one of Owens' cabins: the final death scene, the messy bit, was played out without him some hundreds of feet below it.

The landing stage cleared save for themselves and the attendant, and relieved not to have to think up anything further to say (and perhaps make another gaffe like the one over the cabins), Owens moved quickly forward, beckoning to Sayer to follow him.

Owens called to the attendant, who didn't appear to have noticed the two men waiting on one side. Even when he turned and inclined his head quizzically at Owens, his gaze and interest extended no further than to take in the man who had hailed him.

Owens went up to him; continued to speak in a loud voice. "This gentleman is an investigator from the insurance company, Davey. He wants a word with you about the cabins and the man you let out at the top yesterday morning." Turning back to Sayer, Owens then excused himself for a few moments and went into the control room to speak to Will.

The attendant, who couldn't have been much older than eighteen or nineteen, made no attempt to move; let the insurance investigator approach him. He was wearing blotchy blue jeans and a red anorak which matched his wind-chapped cheeks and hands. His fair hair and ginger beard were close-cropped and curly; and, one would imagine from the purposely insolent look in his eye, going out of his way to be co-operative with the investigator for the guv'nor's insurers would not have been his choice of a good deed for the day.

Sayer went through the usual polite routine he adopted in such circumstances, thanking the young man for his time and assuring him that he wouldn't be detained from his work for a moment longer than necessary. Then he said, "I wonder if you'd mind going through things just one more time for me? I understand that you were working up at the other end yesterday morning."

Davey did not commit himself either way. He slipped his hands into his anorak pockets and leaned back a little on his heels.

There was a pause of something like two or three minutes while he abruptly turned away and attended to a cabin on its return trip down the mountain. He moved round to the other side of the landing stage, discharged the passengers, brought the cabin through the loop and along to where the insurance investigator was standing, then dragged it forward a few feet, swung on it a little, and away it went, empty, back up the mountain. It was all very quick and efficient. He turned back to Sayer, who said, "The first person up to the top yesterday morning, the man: can you describe him for me?"

"No—I told the police yesterday. He vanished, disappeared too quick for me to get a good look at him. It wasn't like he was wearing a big sign round his neck advertising his talent for getting rid of his unwanted lady friends, was it? The cabin hove to; and as I opened the gate, he stepped out—while the cabin was still on the move, as it happened—and without looking at him, I followed through with the cabin to the downside getting it in position ready to be sent back . . . the same drill I went through a few moments ago.

"When I'd done that, got the cabin on its way and turned around, he'd vanished; and the next cabin was coming up, anyway. I didn't give him another thought (why should I—I didn't know there should've been two people in the cabin, did I?). I told you, he was just another man; there was nothing about him to say he was special, different from any of the hundreds of other males I see in and out of the cabins every week."

Sayer said, "Did you see which way he went when he left the landing stage?"

Davey shook his head. "I was busy by that time seeing to the next cabin. There was no one in it, but it still had to be brought round and sent back down again. The cabins are only three or four minutes apart; I don't get time to stand about taking notes. That's not what they pay me for."

"Did he speak?"

Davey shrugged. "He might've; I didn't hear him say anything. The cabins make a fair amount of racket as they sweep up into the landing stage; and I'm not paid—" he scowled "—to hang about making conversation with the customers, either."

Sayer walked to the edge of the landing stage and stood behind a safety rail looking out across the valley.

"Can you see from here the spot where the woman fell from the cabin?" he asked.

It was Owens who moved up and stood beside him and answered his question.

"No. It's the first pylon just beyond that ridge out there." Owens pointed to a ragged slash across the skyline to their right; and Sayer remembered that the ridge had looked quite different, less harsh and forbidding, when viewed from the graveyard in the valley beyond. Owens went on, "That's where we reckon she must've fallen out; either while the cabin lurched through the junction, or immediately afterwards. The cables and pylons cross the valleys in a wide arc, and once you pass over the ridge you disappear from sight. Temporarily, anyway. From that point onwards, you start the ascent up Great Mountain itself in earnest."

Much of that Walsh had told him. Sayer nodded. "I'd like to go on up and take a look, if that's all right with you?"

Owens gestured quickly to Davey, and then ushered Sayer towards the cabin which Davey had just emptied and brought round and was now holding back for him.

Sayer paused to examine the gate and its locking mechanism

before stepping into the cabin and seating himself on a metal bench seat. He deliberately chose to sit facing the way he would be travelling, which put the gate handle at the farthest point from him. Then Sayer watched Davey secure the gate after him.

Like a railway guard walking along a platform slamming open carriage doors, Davey, exercising some considerable force, slammed the cabin gate shut; and then, grabbing hold of a large metal handle on the outside, he gave it a sharp half-turn which locked it.

Sayer did not altogether agree with Walsh over the gate handle, that it wasn't easy to get at from inside the cabin. Difficult to reach, yes, for someone sitting where he was on the hinged side of the gate; but the cabins seated four, two per side facing each other, and anyone seated opposite him would have had only a short reach for it.

So at least one person per cabin could release the gate catch without leaving the safety of his or her seat. But Will—or rather Owens on Will's behalf—had said that the man had sat on the other side, where Sayer was sitting, facing the mountain. It would've been Cynthia Playford who was in the best position for releasing the gate (that was if she'd been sitting up close to it and hadn't moved farther along the seat). The man travelling with her—assuming he had stayed put and hadn't moved at some later stage to sit beside her—would definitely have had to leave his seat to reach the gate handle. But the gate opened outwards. Wouldn't he have risked going out with it?

Sayer revised most of his thinking as he was unceremoniously bumped and bounced like a yo-yo towards the edge of the landing stage ready for takeoff. The nearer he came to that moment, the point of no return, the less likely it seemed to him that the average coward like himself would dream of leaving the security of his seat for *any* reason—to open the gate deliberately (if that was the way Cynthia Playford went out) or to stand up and throw somebody over the side. Fear would paralyse most people into complete immobility. And that, Sayer began to suspect, put the man Walsh was looking for into something of a class of his own: he definitely wasn't your average man in the street, Sayer decided, gritting his teeth as he finally took off.

Where he did agree wholeheartedly with Walsh was that the dead woman would not have willingly stepped through the open gate into fresh air just because someone had asked her to do it. Even if threatened with some kind of weapon, like a knife or a gun, he couldn't see anyone as being that obliging. One glance over the side at the ghastly drop below convinced him of that much.

The cabin steadied and Sayer's stomach caught up with him: it had got left behind at the landing stage where for one or two sickening moments the cabin had been sucked downwards by the tremendous pull of the earth's gravity.

He studied the interior of the cabin and came to the conclusion that with care, someone could change seats from one side to the other while it was in motion. At certain times, that is—like now, while the cabin was in a steady glide; though that person would probably have to be quick about it. He or she would be quite safe, in no real danger of falling out: the cabins were too deep for that to happen accidentally. Any danger there might be was really all in the mind; and it was this, the psychological aspect, that began to intrigue the police officer in Sayer. It made the man Walsh was seeking a much more interesting prospect, somebody who could differentiate between the real danger and the imaginary one and was in complete control of himself at all times (what was it Jones the ticket seller had said about the man . . . something along those lines—that he knew how to handle himself?).

Sayer had reached the ridge, could feel the tremendous upwards surge of man, metal, and machinery as the cabin approached the first pylon. At the junction, the cabin gave a violent jerk, then lurched forward through it, and began the steep ascent up the mountain.

Below him, to his right—dazzling white in a flash of brilliant sunshine and nestling almost at the very foot of the valley—was the graveyard. It had seemed higher up to Sayer than it looked now when viewed by him from aloft. Raising himself slightly from the seat and craning his neck for a better view, he wondered if he would be right in thinking that it had been somewhere hereabouts that Cynthia Playford had plunged to her death.

He looked back over his shoulder at the ridge, but there was no sign as yet of another cabin following him. One passed him, full, on the downside.

At the summit, Sayer stood for a few moments, silent and alone, on a wide plateau made up of muted shades of browns and blacks and greys like the panoramic view which confronted him on all sides. Awesome though it was, the view had more of a subduing effect on him than anything else. He always had an uncomfortable feeling about Welsh mountains, an eerie suspicion that they were standing there looking at him in an even less favourable light than he was looking at them.

He spoke first to the anxious little man who prowled up and down the length of the stationary green-and-white Council-operated cable car selling tickets for the ride down the windward side of the mountain. Yes, he had been on duty all yesterday morning (well, up until eleven-thirty or thereabouts when the police had arrived and everything had come to a complete standstill); but no, he had no recollection of seeing a man in a grey-maybe-fawn raincoat (tartan-lined), though he admitted that it was quite possible that the man, if he had waited around out of sight until just before eleven o'clock when things had started to get busy, could have been amongst the first couple of carloads of people to be taken back down the mountain. He just didn't notice him, that's all. The driver of the cable car was equally unhelpful.

Sayer did not bother to wait around for the café to open at eleven. Walsh had described its coffee as being diabolical, and there seemed little point in questioning the staff. Walsh had already drawn a complete blank there. Nobody could remember seeing any man matching the description Will had given the police—with or without a grey or fawn tartan-lined raincoat or possibly with a long woollen scarf wound round his head to keep out the chill mountain air. It did not seem particularly relevant now to Sayer, anyway; what or who the café staff could or could not remember seeing yesterday morning. While, obviously, it went without saying that he would have liked to know more about the man who had shared Cynthia Playford's cabin ride, there was little doubt in his mind how she had met her end; and it was not by accident. His brief went no further than to absolve the cabin-lift operator of any negligence; and Sayer simply did not feel he could justify the spending of any more of his time and the insurance company's money on the matter, despite his natural inclination as a former high-ranking police officer to want to search out the full answer to the riddle of the woman's death. That was up to Walsh and he was best left to get on with it, Sayer acknowledged with a small sigh of regret. He would call in at The Grand and say good-bye to Walsh and then get back home to those weeds he had promised faithfully he would rid the garden of over the long holiday weekend.

The cable car was quickly filling up with passengers. Sayer bought a ticket and joined them.

CHAPTER 9

Sayer stopped short. Reception was crammed to overflowing with women of all shapes and sizes—young, old, and in-between. More kept arriving by the second, coming, he noted, from the direction of the ballroom.

He pressed on; glanced at the time—a few minutes after eleven —then at the notice board listing the day's events, wondering if he would find an explanation somewhere there for all this unexpected feminine activity. . . .

| 10:00 A.M. | Wellington Room: | Lecture on Magic for Children by John Manders. |
| | Ballroom: | Ladies' Event, Lecture on Clairvoyance and Fortune Telling by Madame Adele Herrmann. |

Sayer had barely finished reading the details of the ladies' event when he heard her voice. He turned. Her lecture over, Edwina Charles—or Madame Adele Herrmann as she was known professionally—was with the last of the magicians' wives to leave the ballroom. She did not notice Sayer for the moment; and then, when finally their eyes met, he had the satisfaction, for the first time ever in their long association with one another, of seeing her taken completely by surprise.

Mrs. Charles hesitated, smiled, and then making some excuse to the two women with her, walked over to him. "Why, Superintendent. What a pleasant surprise. Fancy seeing you here!"

"You took the words right out of my mouth," he replied, smiling back at her.

Not really beautiful, the clairvoyante was nevertheless a handsome woman, with short, feathery gold hair and a complexion which was as wrinkle-free as when they had first met. He had never been sure of her age. She had turned forty; further than that he was not prepared to commit himself.

He studied her face closely. There was something different about it. She looked tired and strained, but he put that down to the lecture she had just given. Something else. The voice was the same. The smile . . .

An uneasy feeling came over him, a feeling he had experienced before when finding himself confronted by the clairvoyante in similar circumstances. Previously when a murder investigation had brought them together, either by design or, as in this instance, quite by chance, she had succeeded in concealing her true thoughts and feelings from him, but this time they were laid bare. She was very upset about something—deeply distressed, he realised with a sudden shock.

"Shall we find somewhere quiet to sit and talk, and perhaps have some coffee?" he suggested.

She nodded; indicated an anteroom behind him. "That small lounge over there, I think. The Wellington Room will be rather crowded at the moment. The men's lecture has just finished, and I understand there's to be a brief church service held in there shortly."

There were only three other people in the side lounge off reception; two of them were reading newspapers, the third taking a nap.

"Well, Superintendent," said Mrs. Charles when they had settled themselves comfortably in a quiet corner and given their order to the waitress. "What brings you to Plaid-yro-Wyth?"

He told her; watched her blue eyes darken as he had seen them do on other occasions when something was troubling her.

"But it wasn't an accident," she said when he had finished.

"No, Madame," he said gravely. "Fortunately not—that is, so far as my employers, the cabin-lift operator's insurers, are concerned."

The clairvoyante sighed. "I warned Cynthia not to come. Begged her to let her brother make this trip alone."

"You knew Cynthia Playford?" Sayer looked surprised. His eyebrows rose interrogatively. "Professionally?"

"If by that you mean, was she a client, the answer is yes. It was also through Cynthia and her brother, Nigel, that I was invited by the Mystic Circle to lecture here this weekend to the magicians' wives while their menfolk were otherwise occupied."

"Are the police aware of your professional relationship with the dead woman?"

"Possibly . . . I don't really know. Her brother might've told them, though I doubt it—I don't believe they've interviewed him, not properly. A plainclothes detective sergeant and a uniformed police officer spent yesterday afternoon in the hotel taking statements from various people, but neither of them spoke to me. In any event," the clairvoyante went on after a small pause, "the police are bound to discover the counsellor-client relationship which existed between Cynthia and myself. For the past six months, Cynthia had been consulting me regularly once a month at my home, and I know she kept a record of her appointments with me in the diary she always carried with her."

Sayer was frowning. "Which name did she put in the diary? Your professional name?"

Mrs. Charles smiled faintly at the expression on his face. He looked most concerned. "I didn't kill Cynthia Playford, Superintendent. I have nothing to fear."

"Perish the thought," he said quickly. "It was just that as an ex–police officer—"

"I quite understand," she interrupted him with a solemn nod. "I know only too well how easily these simple, innocent things can become distorted and misinterpreted, and get out of hand. To Cynthia I was always Madame—Madame Herrmann—and this was the name she noted down in her diary."

"So the police are definitely going to want to talk to you fairly soon," he said slowly. "That's if the diary was amongst the things she brought with her this weekend."

Mrs. Charles made no comment.

"May I ask why she was consulting you?"

Again the clairvoyante smiled at the look of concern on his face. "The police aren't looking for a woman in connection with the crime, are they? I understood—or rather, rumour has it— they're looking for a man in a mackintosh . . . some kind of un- usual raincoat."

"Frankly, Madame, I don't think they really know what they're looking for. I know the senior police officer in charge of the case—an able enough copper on routine investigations, but a bit of a plodder, and this one's tricky. He's moving too slowly; letting the scent go cold. . . ."

"Or in other words," she said with a wry smile, "if you were in charge of the investigation, you'd have long since interviewed me."

"Yes, Madame," he admitted. "If I'd got my hands on her diary, you would've been one of the first people I'd have wanted to interview."

"Then I'm afraid you'd be disappointed with the results," she said and gave him a very thoughtful look. "There's very little that I'll be able to tell the police that they won't get from her brother. He and Cynthia were very close. Abnormally so," she added with a small, dismissive gesture.

He looked at her searchingly. "Was this why she was consult- ing you?"

The clairvoyante frowned. "It was part of her problem, but not the whole picture. Cynthia Playford was an extremely com- plex person whose emotional troubles, I believe, stemmed— though she would've been the first to deny it—from her child- hood. Her parents were involved in a particularly sordid—for its day, that is—divorce action when she and Nigel were quite small children. Their father ran off with some other woman, and their mother raised them on her own—had quite a hard time of it, by all accounts. Nigel and Cynthia were devoted to her, and she to them; and then when she died, Cynthia reacted by embarking upon a long series of affairs with married men, all of whom were head over heels in love with her, deliberately creating—one couldn't help but feel—a situation between her current lover and herself and her lover's wife similar to the one which her father had created between himself, his wife, and his mistress. But with one curious anomaly: it was always Cynthia who ultimately backed away from the situation. Until six months ago—"

"She finally wanted to marry somebody who wouldn't divorce his wife for her?" guessed Sayer. Then, in response to the clairvoyante's faint nod: "And what did she expect you to do for her?"

"The usual." The clairvoyante looked quite grim. "She wanted me to tell her the only thing she wanted to hear—that there was going to be a happy ending to her story. Nobody with a problem goes to a clairvoyante to hear the truth, Superintendent. They already know what that is." She paused and sighed. "I'm sorry if that sounds cynical; but sometimes—just once—I wish people like Cynthia Playford (those who consult me) would listen to the advice I give them. Unfortunately, they're basically all the same, self-destructive. If Cynthia had listened to me, taken my advice, waited, been patient, then everything would have worked out for her. . . ."

"Romantically speaking, I take it?"

"Yes," she replied, ignoring the sarcasm heavily overlaying his query. She was thoughtful for a moment. "I spoke to Cynthia over the telephone earlier in the week in connection with my lecture today, and it was obvious to me then that she was breaking down under the severe strain which the emotional entanglement in her private life was imposing on her. Her conversation was disjointed—at times her mind would go completely blank in the middle of a sentence and she'd have no idea what she was saying or what she'd intended to say. There were moments when I wondered if she even knew to whom she was speaking. She wasn't due to see me again until Friday of this coming week, and I urged her in the meanwhile to take a complete rest from everything. That was why I advised her so strongly against coming here this weekend. She was at the breaking point, Superin-

tendent. The slightest thing—the most trivial of emotional upsets
—would have pushed her right over the edge into a complete
mental and physical breakdown."

"Well, she went over the edge, all right," he observed grimly.
"But not into a breakdown. To her death."

"No, Superintendent, you're wrong there . . . about the mental breakdown. When I spoke to her yesterday morning, it was
very apparent to me from her general demeanour that she'd
finally broken down. I had just arrived; and she was on her way
out, it would now seem, to keep her appointment with death.
We spoke briefly over there—" the clairvoyante nodded in the direction of the reception desk "—and it was much the same thing
as before. She was completely and utterly distracted; her conversation was again inclined to be vague and disjointed, and she
didn't appear generally to know whether she was coming or
going. Quite honestly, in retrospect, most of what she said made
little or no sense at all. And then—again in one of those midsen-
tence blanks of hers—she abruptly excused herself with the
promise that we would lunch together and talk some more then.
That was the last I saw of her."

"She made no mention of where she was going?"

The clairvoyante shook her head. Then, after a slight hesita-
tion: "My impression now is that she had something very
definite in mind, like an appointment she was afraid she might
be late in keeping. Yes," she said slowly, "with hindsight, I
would say she was definitely on her way to meet somebody, as
I've said, by appointment."

Sayer, on hearing Walsh's unmistakable voice as the latter
passed through reception, suddenly decided that the weeds in
his garden would have to wait. He smiled at the waitress who
brought their coffee and tipped her generously, perhaps in grati-
tude for his having found a legitimate excuse for avoiding his
gardening chores, which he loathed. He knew his wife, Jean,
would approve of his decision to remain in Plaid-yro-Wyth and
his reasons for doing so. Walsh might or might not ultimately
make the connection between the deceased and the women's lec-

turer hired by the magic society, and if and when he did, Sayer wanted to be there. Not simply because he considered himself to be the clairvoyante's friend—and she could well need a friend, someone to talk to, before the weekend was over: as a former police officer, he considered it his duty to make sure that Walsh recognised the woman's potential, that uncanny ability of hers—which Sayer had seen demonstrated time and again on those other murder investigations in which they had found themselves jointly involved—to see the not-so-obvious, and that Walsh used it to its full advantage. Sayer knew from personal experience that Walsh would dismiss her as a crackpot. He also knew, again from personal experience, that in that event it would be the biggest mistake Walsh could make; and from his observations of Walsh's handling of the case to date, Walsh had already made quite a few.

Two elderly women had approached Mrs. Charles while Sayer was preoccupied with the waitress—a Mrs. Toomey and Mrs. Belson, he heard them introduce themselves as. As the waitress turned away, they, or rather Mrs. Toomey, who appeared to have elected herself spokeswoman on their joint behalf, was explaining to the clairvoyante that they were not with the convention, but had been graciously permitted by the convention organisers to attend her lecture and would now very much like to consult her that afternoon between two and three when Mrs. Charles was apparently giving private readings. They seemed delighted—Mrs. Toomey, in particular—when the clairvoyante assured them both that it would be her pleasure and thanked her profusely.

"What on earth would a couple of dear old biddies like that hope to hear from a fortune teller?" inquired Sayer when the two women were out of earshot.

"They both have very sick husbands," said the clairvoyante. "I would expect them to be seeking some reassurance in that direction."

"You could tell all that—about their husbands—just by looking at them?" he asked, wide-eyed.

Mrs. Charles smiled. "You do wonders for my ego, Superintendent. I only wsh I could say yes; but unfortunately, I overheard someone discussing them and their respective spouses at breakfast this morning."

"You're very honest, Madame," he said with a rueful grin.

She gave him a thoughtful look. "It's the best policy, Superintendent. Haven't you heard?"

CHAPTER 10

The small side room known as the Marlborough Room, which the hotel management had made available to Chief Inspector Walsh and his team, had originally been intended for use by the convention committee principally as the registration office. The relevant signs had therefore been taken down and transferred from there—together with the quarter-filled cardboard boxes of numbered envelopes containing a day-by-day programme of events, name badge, and other paraphernalia relating to the convention which were handed out to every conventioneer as he or she registered—to a quiet corner of the Wellington Room where a table and chairs had been set up and latecomers could now register for the weekend.

The president of the Mystic Circle, Lance Headley, was all for cancelling the function; but Nigel Playford had refused to hear of it. There was the expense everyone had gone to: that, he felt, should be taken into consideration before any rush decision to cancel was made; there was also the competition on Sunday and the disappointment of the contestants after months of preparation for the event; and after consulting with the local CID and the hotel management, the convention committee had decided, in deference to Nigel's wishes, that the convention would continue as planned.

Walsh was sure it had been the right decision to make in the circumstances. Most of the conventioneers would have to remain in Plaid-yro-Wyth for the remainder of Easter Sunday, anyway—some possibly overnight—while he got round to seeing them; and in the meanwhile, it was far better that they and their thoughts were kept fully occupied with their consuming interest in magic rather than with the murder investigation that was now an addendum to the convention agenda.

The conventioneers themselves were divided over the issue; the magic dealers, at least one of whom was overheard by Walsh expressing his relief that the function was not to be called off, were wholeheartedly for it. Business, Walsh gathered, was not too good in the magic trade at the moment. He wondered that there was a living in selling magic tricks: with one or two exceptions, the dealers all appeared to be selling the same items in direct competition with one another and, so far as Walsh could see, to a very limited market. But as Lance Headley pointed out to him, most of the dealers were professional entertainers in their own right; magic dealing was only a sideline. Just as well, thought Walsh.

Headley, as president of the society, personally escorted the Chief Inspector round the dealers' room while they were waiting for the interdenominational church service which was being conducted in the Wellington Room to come to a close.

Walsh had deliberately delayed interviewing anyone connected with the convention, including the deceased's brother, until he had had an opportunity to study the pathologist's findings; and this he did over a hurried working lunch of egg-and-watercress sandwiches and tea after he had finished looking round the magic dealers.

"Makes interesting reading, doesn't it?" he remarked as Sayer, who had joined him for lunch, finished going through the pathologist's report and slipped it back inside the grey folder in which it had been presented to Walsh. "Specifically that bit about a recent abortion and the sterilization op."

Walsh had not questioned Sayer's continuing presence in Plaid-yro-Wyth. Knowing that Sayer had been forced to retire from the force through ill health—a near fatal coronary—he thought he could understand how the former Detective Chief Superintendent must be feeling. Extremely nostalgic, Walsh would imagine, for the old days.

There was a light tap on the door, and raising his eyebrows, Walsh murmured, "That'll probably be Playford now."

Sayer gathered their lunch things together and stacked them on the ornately carved mantelshelf to the right of Walsh's desk, then crossed to the door and opened it.

With his creased, pink, podgy face, weak red-rimmed blue eyes, and wide gaping mouth, Nigel reminded Sayer of an unborn piglet. Nigel looked bemused, not yet fully awake. He had sat up all night, to begin with alone with Frank and Kath Sexton; then later Lance Headley had joined them. Nobody had uttered a word throughout the entire night; and then at seven in the morning, almost as if by some secret signal that the wake was at an end and they were now excused, Headley had stood up, given Nigel's arm a quick, sympathetic squeeze, and slipped back to his room to shower and change before breakfast; then Frank and Kath Sexton had got to their feet and likewise disappeared.

Nigel had come straight from the church service, which made the need for him to be carrying a raincoat rather puzzling—unless, thought Walsh whimsically, it had been raining in the Wellington Room, or Playford intended to go out for a walk once he was through with him.

The raincoat was folded neatly over Nigel's right arm as if he were indeed on his way out somewhere. An expensive coat, fawn, and of the type made famous by a certain former British Prime Minister. It had a red tartan lining. Nigel, in arranging the garment over the leather armchair just inside the door, seemed concerned to see to it that no one should miss this little detail. It was a curious pantomime and Walsh watched Nigel's performance with interest. *Well, well, well, so word had got around about the coat!* The Chief Inspector guessed that this might have been the message Nigel was trying to get across to him.

Walsh indicated where Nigel should seat himself. Sayer was standing on Nigel's left, with his back to the fireplace. Walsh offered no explanation for Sayer's presence, and Nigel assumed he was merely another plainclothes detective.

Almost immediately Nigel started to talk in a nervous babble about the protracted church service, how it had gone on for much longer than anyone had expected due to the lengthy tribute paid by the minister—a Mystic Circle member and conventioneer like himself, and a close personal friend—to his sister; and Walsh gave him his head until finally, the quietness of the other two men in the room suddenly registered with Nigel and he rather began to suspect that he was carrying on like an idiot, probably not making much sense, and checked himself.

"Sorry," he said shortly. Then, by way of explanation: "For going on like that. Shock, I guess. I still can't believe it, that she's gone. God—" he said dramatically and cast his eyes upwards, blinking rapidly. "Why did I say those things to her? I was only kidding; I just wanted to make her mad." He looked back at Walsh and shook his head. "I admit she hadn't been looking too well lately, but I had no idea she was so low—depressed, I mean. Beamish wasn't worth dying for. How could she do it, take her life over a creep like him?"

Walsh cleared his throat and shifted about on his chair as if to ease a growing stiffness in his posterior. "That's what you think happened to your sister, Mr. Playford? She committed suicide?"

"Well, it was certainly no accident; I can tell you that much," replied Nigel bitterly.

"Were you aware that your sister planned to go up to the summit of Great Mountain via the cabin lift first thing yesterday morning?" inquired Walsh.

Nigel shook his head and frowned. "She must've made up her mind on the spur of the moment—after breakfast—and then simply went ahead and did it." He gulped a little, appalled by the wider implications of what he had just said.

Walsh picked up a pencil and then holding it in both hands, elbows on the desk, he twisted it slowly backwards and forwards between his fingertips. "The man who was with your sister yesterday morning, Mr. Playford, have you any idea who he might've been?"

Nigel gave him a puzzled look. "Nobody said anything to me about a man. What man?"

"I was rather hoping," said Walsh, "that you would be able to tell me who he was, not the other way round. This isn't a general knowledge quiz. I've only got the questions, not the answers." He laid the pencil on the desk and leaned back resignedly in his chair; got out his handkerchief and used it. "Your sister shared the cabin she intended to ride in up to the summit with a man."

Nigel was shaking his head. Then an odd expression crossed his face. "Something my sister said to me while we were driving here on Friday. . . ." He paused and Walsh waited to let him get it right. Walsh had a shrewd suspicion that Nigel was up to something—what exactly Walsh wasn't sure. But he doubted that Nigel was being completely straightforward with him.

Nigel's eyebrows rose interrogatively. "Do you have a description of this man?"

"Yes, and from what we've been told about him, Mr. Playford, one couldn't be blamed for thinking it might've been you." Walsh pointedly considered Nigel's silver-blond head of hair, tried to picture it concealed under a woollen scarf. "Give or take one or two minor discrepancies here and there," the Chief Inspector added dryly. "You are perhaps a shade shorter than the man whose description we've been given—"

Walsh was glancing through a sheaf of papers in the open file in front of him. He removed one of the sheets and read it for a moment. "You were at a band call yesterday morning between nine-thirty and eleven—" he frowned, used his handkerchief again "—a rehearsal for a competition that's to be held later this afternoon?"

He looked up when there was no response from Nigel, who seemed lost in thought.

Walsh lengthened his gaze from the intently thoughtful man seated before him to include the armchair near the door. The raincoat puzzled him. Playford was definitely playing some kind of game with him over it; Playford could afford to take the risk that his little game might suddenly backfire on him because he knew his alibi for the time of his sister's murder was sound. But what were his motives? Why had he pretended—not very con-

vincingly at that—to know nothing about the man who had been
seen with his sister yesterday morning? He knew about one—the
man's raincoat—so he knew about the other. Had to. Walsh made
a bet with himself. Playford knew who it was, and the name of
the game was "misdirection." Every word Playford said, every
action he made, had but one purpose: to lead him up the garden
path.

Nigel's head suddenly moved slowly up and down. "Beamish—
Dr. Henry Beamish," he said. "If you're looking for someone
who looks a bit like me, then he's your man. He's taller than I am
too."

"That's the second time you've mentioned that name," said
Walsh, blowing his nose vigorously. "Who is he?"

"My sister's ex-lover. She told me she'd finished with him; it
was all over between them. I didn't believe her, but I guess she
really meant it after all. He must've followed us here and arranged to meet her yesterday to talk things over." Nigel rested
an arm on the desk, leaned forward earnestly, and frowned.
"Cynthia knew how I felt about him, so that was why she didn't
say anything to me about going out."

Nigel withdrew his arm from the desk and clasped his hands
between his knees. Then, in a bewildered, little-boy-lost voice:
"So it's true what everybody's been trying not to say to me for
the past twenty-four hours. Cynthia didn't commit suicide; she
was murdered. That bastard Beamish killed her." He threw back
his head and laughed at the ceiling. "God, it's incredible!" He
looked back at Walsh and his eyes became fixed and staring.
"Do you know what Cynthia said to me about him, that creep,
Beamish . . . what, less than forty-eight hours ago?" His face
contorted and flushed a dark shade of red. (Now, thought
Walsh, we're seeing the real man.) "She said Henry Beamish
was the only man she'd ever really loved."

Walsh said quietly, "Why, then, do you suppose, did she end
their affair?"

Nigel looked bewildered and distressed, and Walsh was again
struck by the same thought: that this, at last, was the real Nigel

Playford, saying what he really thought and felt, no more fun and games.

"I don't know," said Nigel, shaking his head. "None of it makes any sense. Particularly that . . . that she should be the one to end it. That wasn't her style. Cynthia never ended anything in her life."

"Your sister had had other lovers?"

"Yes," said Nigel matter-of-factly. "But Cynthia herself never finished with any of them. She always let the little woman do that. It was the way she got her kicks." He smiled crookedly. "My sister wasn't your average female . . . er, Chief Inspector, isn't it? You'll find that out, though, soon enough."

Walsh said, "By 'the little woman' I assume you mean there was usually a wife somewhere on the scene."

"Usually?" Nigel laughed a derisory *hah! "Always!* Cynthia loved it, being the third side of the eternal triangle, pushing the wife to the end of her endurance, humiliating her and then sitting back and waiting to see what she'd do about it. It's a marvel to me that this didn't happen sooner—" he shrugged "—except that it's all wrong, back to front . . . the way it happened, I mean. It shouldn't have been one of her ex-lovers who killed her." His mouth twisted in what might or might not have been meant to be a smile. "And you know something, I bet that came as a shock to her too: one hell of a disappointment that her killer wasn't one of her ex-victims, some poor woman whose nose she'd rubbed in it. She really had the knife into them. That is, it always seemed that way to me. Though why beats me. I've never been able to figure it out. Something to do with the bust-up between our parents?" He shrugged, looked perplexed. "That was over another woman. Perhaps Cynthia was scarred deeper by it than anyone imagined."

He paused, shrugged again, and then went on in the same vein, talking more to himself. "Maybe she hated our mother for letting some other woman take our father from us. That could've been why it was always the same old scene played over and over again . . . plunging the wife into the depths of despair and humiliation to see how much she'd take and at what point the worm would turn and start dishing out the same kind of treatment to her. They did in the end, you know. Turn. Every single one of them. It was always the wife who ended the affair and gave Cynthia the royal order of the boot."

"Can you think of any reason why this Dr. Beamish should've been different?"

Nigel widened his eyes and shook his head. "None at all. I told you, it's weird; none of it makes any sense to me."

"He was married, I take it?"

Nigel nodded. "He fitted the norm—the pattern, that is," he added sardonically, "to which Cynthia always worked. Wealthy wife, the devoted, clinging type. . . ."

"Dr. Beamish," said Walsh and eyed Nigel speculatively. "A literary man—university professor?" he guessed.

Nigel said sourly, "No, nothing so special. The usual common or garden-variety doctor. And it's *mister,* not doctor." The crooked smile was back. "My little joke at good old Henry's expense."

"Specialist?"

"A gynaecologist, no less," sneered Nigel.

"Was that how he and your sister met? Through a doctor-patient relationship?"

"You're joking! Cynthia never had a day's sickness in her entire life. She didn't believe in it. Sickness. A person was either alive or dead. There was no in-between with her."

"She didn't consult Dr.—*Mr.*—Beamish, say for example, because she was pregnant and wished to procure an abortion?"

Nigel laughed. "No, she met Beamish at some charity fundraising bash or other." He laughed again and shook his head. "Cyn pregnant! You've got to be joking. She'd have killed herself first!"

"No, Mr. Playford," said Walsh quietly. He got out his handkerchief and used it again. "She didn't do that; she took the more usual course—usual, that is, for today."

A slight frown on Nigel's forehead developed into a deep,

harsh groove. Then he shook his head quickly. "Never," he said emphatically. "I don't believe it!"

Walsh referred to the pathologist's report, read in silence for a moment, then looked up again at Nigel. "Approximately two months ago, Mr. Playford, your sister underwent an abortion. The termination was followed up with a routine sterilization operation. According to the medical examiner's findings on the postmortem he carried out on your sister yesterday afternoon, there was no evidence of any complication following either surgical procedure."

Nigel leaned forward in his chair. He spoke urgently. "My sister was going to have Henry Beamish's child?"

"If you say so, Mr. Playford," said Walsh evenly.

CHAPTER 11

Stunned, Walsh's voice ringing loudly in his ears, Nigel stood in the corridor outside the Marlborough Room; then almost as if suddenly afraid that the door would open and someone would appear and find him hanging about out there, he darted quickly forward towards the Wellington Room. At the door, he paused and looked in. Kath had said she would wait for him there.

They spotted one another at the same moment, Kath jumping up instantly from the settee where she had been sitting alone watching anxiously for him and then tagging on to the tail end of the slow-moving, noisy group of people drifting towards the door. Her face was waxen, and there were dark grainy stains under her eyes. She was very tense: she started to speak well before she reached him and he held up a hand, frowned a quick warning, and cut in on her. "Where's Frank?" he asked. "Gone in for lunch?"

Kath hesitated, closed her eyes, and put a hand to her forehead and held it there. He stepped forward swiftly and took her arm to steady her. "Come on, old thing," he said, frowning. He looked round uncomfortably to see how much notice was being taken of them. None that he could see. The room had almost cleared; only half a dozen or so stragglers remained, those who had either yet to experience the poor waitress service in the dining room or were quite unconcerned by it and didn't mind anything up to an hour's wait, if one were amongst the latecomers, for their first orders to be taken.

Nigel increased the pressure of his hand on Kath's arm and gave her a gentle shake. "It's not as bad as all that. I'm pretty sure I fooled them." Perspiration beaded his forehead, and he

had an excess of bitter-tasting saliva in his mouth which he
didn't seem to be able to get rid of, no matter how many times or
how hard he swallowed. "Let's get a breath of fresh air. We'll
talk outside."

Kath studied him closely. He looked dreadful. Something was
wrong: they had told him something in there—about Frank—that
had upset him badly. She swallowed the panic rising like a
scream in her throat and made herself say, reasonably calmly,
"What are we going to do about it, Nigel—Frank's raincoat?"

"Shush," he said, propelling her past the reception desk and
the mildly interested glances of the Toomeys who had been out
for a walk and were now waiting for the receptionist to fetch
them their room key.

Nigel fed Kath into the revolving door to the street, then himself. Once they were through it, he said, "We've already been
through all that, Kath. The coat's *mine.*"

"But did the police *ask* you if it were yours?" she persisted.

"Would you bother if you saw me carrying it over my arm?"
He squeezed her arm again and smiled—but not at her, she noticed. He was looking everywhere *but* at her. He went on, still
smiling, "Married to a magician all these years and you still
don't know the first basic rule, the simple art of misdirection?"

Kath looked at him anxiously. What was wrong? Why
couldn't, *wouldn't,* he look her in the eye? *"Oh, God, no . . .
Frank, Frank!"* a little voice inside her screamed. Then, in a
slow, controlled voice, she said, "I still think I should've got rid
of it, driven out into the country somewhere and dumped it. I
shouldn't have dragged you into this. . . ."

Nigel was beginning to agree with her. He liked Kath, always
had; felt he owed her something for the humiliating way
Cynthia had treated her. Nothing would bring Cynthia back:
God knows why that fool Sexton had killed her or what had happened between them over the phone on Friday night which had
led to all this; but whatever it was, there was no getting away
from the fact that Cynthia had created her own epitaph, as so
often happens with her kind. Her philosophy that people only

get what they deserve had finally been extended far enough to include herself; and he wasn't too sure now that this hadn't been the way she had always planned it. That she too would one day get what she deserved and be a victim of herself, though heaven only knows if she had meant it to go this far. Perhaps she had. He didn't know, didn't understand anything any more. He just knew he couldn't let it go any further; this was where it had to stop. Cynthia had had her pound of flesh. Enough was enough. He didn't give a damn about Sexton. The police could hang, draw, and quarter him for all he cared. But where would that leave Kath? Where she'd always been, where Cynthia had put her. In the victim's chair.

"Look, Kath," Nigel sighed. "We don't know that it was Frank. We don't know that it was anybody. Maybe the police aren't very busy right now and are just looking for something to do to pass the time. You'll see—" He tried to smile, but his face wouldn't work. "They'll find out that that country bumpkin they've got up there oiling turnstiles, or whatever it is he does, was mistaken. Cynthia took her own life. And—" He hesitated, hoped his voice wasn't betraying what he really felt and believed and how much he pitied Kath. "Something they've just told me convinces me of it."

She shot him a quick look, but he shook his head at the question he read in her eyes. How could he tell her—*anyone*—that Cynthia and that . . . that *slime*—?

Nigel made himself stop, pressed a handkerchief quickly to his lips, and dabbed at his sweaty brow. "The least you know, Kath, the better; then when it's your turn to see the police you won't suddenly find yourself in a position where you've got to tell lies."

They had made their way round the cars parked on the forecourt and crossed the street to an undulating lawned square. The sun was shining and surprisingly warm, so the few places where one could sit and bask were all taken. Without talking, they did a turn of the square, and on the second time round they found themselves a vacant wooden bench to sit on.

Nigel sat staring at the cream and gold daffodils growing wild round the trunk of a dainty young silver birch, not yet in full leaf, standing at the edge of the gravelled footpath to the front of them. He could still hear Walsh's voice. . . . Lies, *filthy* lies! None of it was true—any moment now he would wake up and the nightmare would be over. Beamish wasn't any different from the rest—*he wasn't!*—it was all a dirty lie. Cynthia would have told him about it, the baby. They never kept secrets. *Never!*

Kath broke the silence. "I'm scared silly, Nigel. Terrified," she whispered. "Frank still won't tell me where he went yesterday morning. And we both know—everybody does—that Cynthia wanted to talk to him about something. Why else did she ring down for him to come to the phone on Friday night?" She paused and bit momentarily into her bottom lip. "He's going to confess, Nigel; I can tell by his eyes. Something . . . something's died in him, with . . . her." She tried but couldn't bring herself to couple her husband's name with Cynthia's. Not even for Nigel's sake. "It doesn't matter to him any more; he doesn't care if he's arrested. I think he'd welcome it."

She frowned at Nigel and became a little alarmed. Frank always said Nigel had never grown up, and for the first time she could see in Nigel's face what Frank had meant. Nigel was like a small boy who had been severely punished for something he hadn't done and who, overwhelmed by the injustice of it, was withdrawing into himself. "Are you all right, Nigel?" Her voice softened with concern and pity for him. "What is it?"

He looked at her, then down, distractedly, at the handkerchief balled in his fist. Sweat was trickling down his neck and staining his shirt collar. "I feel—" he began. Then, shocked: "Christ, Kath, I think I'm going to be sick!"

Henry Beamish paused at the ninth hole of his ritual Sunday morning round of golf to talk to the corpulent young detective sergeant from the Plaid-yro-Wyth CID. Beamish's friends played on, leaving him to catch them up as best he could.

He was of medium height and build, running perhaps a little to fat, sandy-haired under a jaunty white-peaked cap (age about fifty, Sergeant Rhys-Williams supposed), and wore a bright red pullover over a white open-neck shirt and light grey tailored flannel slacks. A large gold filling partially capped his right incisor, though the overall evenness and whiteness of his teeth rather suggested that they were dentures with the gold capping for cosmetic purposes only.

If one stood up close and took each of his physical features and examined them individually, then Nigel could have been said to be deluding himself, even accused of deliberately trying to mislead the police; he and Henry Beamish looked nothing alike. A quick overall glance, though, and there was a vague similarity between the two men, enough to make those who were slightly acquainted with either of them pause and take a second look.

Beamish spoke and moved with ease and an unhurried grace. A very successful man who knew his worth, Rhys-Williams noted not without some envy.

"We could let this wait until you get back to the clubhouse, sir," he suggested politely.

"No, it's all right, Sergeant," Beamish assured him. "I doubt if I'll last the distance, anyway. My shoulder's giving me a spot of bother today. I sprained it slightly while I was working in my garden yesterday. It won't hurt to give it a rest for a few minutes while we talk." He exercised his injured shoulder for a moment, then moodily chivvied a piece of loose turf with the head of his number two wood. "There's just one thing, though, Sergeant, before we take this conversation any further. I feel I should make my position absolutely clear—" he looked up quickly "—I'm assuming, of course, that it's one of my patients you wish to discuss with me; in which case, I'm sorry to be a bore, but you know how it is—"

Rhys-Williams said quickly, "Yes, of course, I understand perfectly, sir. But I don't think this lady was one of your patients. At least that's not our information."

Leaning on the club, the gynaecologist shaded out the bright sunlight with his left hand and gazed into the distance at the shot one of his friends had just made. "My God, did you see that? I'd die happy if just once I could hit a ball like that." He dropped his arm and looked at Rhys-Williams. "I'm sorry— You were saying?"

"Miss Cynthia Playford?"

Beamish narrowed his eyes. "Yes," he said warily. "What about her?"

"I understand that you and Miss Playford were quite good friends, sir."

All signs of Beamish's former amicability vanished. His face hardened. So did his voice. "Get to the point please, Sergeant. You know all this or you wouldn't be here spoiling my game." His sudden smile, a rather cruel one, was highlighted by the gold on his capped incisor. "Well, what mischief has the wilful Miss Playford been up to this time? Nothing nice, I'll be bound."

"Miss Playford is dead, sir," Rhys-Williams informed him. "It happened yesterday morning. I thought you knew . . . When I phoned your home earlier this morning from Plaid-yro-Wyth, the lady I spoke to said she'd tell—"

Beamish cut in abruptly. "I'd already left when you rang. The message that you wished to see me sometime this morning was relayed to me by one of the club stewards." Beamish's eyes were downcast, fixed on a tiny disturbed sod of earth which he pressed firmly back into place with the toe of his right shoe. "How much did you tell my wife?" he asked.

"Actually very little, sir. Mrs. Beamish rather took me un-awares. She seemed to know why we wanted to talk to you. This morning's papers, I daresay. Miss Playford's death got a mention in most of them."

"I haven't got round to looking at any of them yet," said Beamish curtly. "I don't usually, not until after lunch." He frowned at the sergeant. "Did my wife seem at all distressed when you spoke to her?"

"I don't think so, sir. Though I can't be sure about that. It's not always easy to tell over the phone."

Beamish dropped the club he'd been toying with into his golf bag. "I think I'd better get on home to her, if you don't mind, Sergeant. This is bound to upset her. We can talk as we walk to my car."

They fell into step. After a moment or two's silence, Rhys-Williams said, "Were you aware, sir, that Miss Playford had recently had an abortion?"

"Yes," replied Beamish in a clipped tone. "Next question. . . . No, spare me that one, please; let me save you the bother. Yes, it was my child."

"Was it Miss Playford's decision to have an abortion?"

"No, mine. She wanted to go ahead and have the child. But it was quite out of the question. My wife is dying, Sergeant; she has less than six months to live. I'd hurt her enough. I couldn't do that to her, couldn't let my mistress go ahead and bear the child my wife had always wanted and never been able to have."

"What if Miss Playford had felt differently?"

Beamish shot the sergeant an irritable look. "Fortunately, she didn't. She was an intelligent woman—at least, I'd always thought so—and when I explained the situation to her, that my wife hadn't long to go and that she (Miss Playford) just had to be patient, there'd be other children, marriage—all the things we both wanted—Miss Playford eventually saw reason and agreed to comply with my wishes on the matter. We also agreed that we should discontinue our relationship for the time being."

"The sterilization operation?" inquired Rhys-Williams, and Beamish hesitated midstride. "Who's idea, then, was that, sir?" finished the sergeant.

Beamish stared at him. "Nonsense," he said after a moment. Then slowly, doubtfully: "Cynthia wouldn't have been so wilfully stupid."

"According to the pathologist's report," Rhys-Williams intoned with a suddenly pronounced Welsh lilt, "a sterilization operation was performed on Miss Playford at or around the time of the abortion."

"That vindictive, self-destructive little bitch!" Beamish spat out vehemently. Then, remembering himself, he shrugged and said, "But then again, I don't know why I should be so surprised. It's just the sort of thing she would do." He smiled his cruel smile. "The abortion must've really thrown her off balance."

"Aren't most women pretty upset about it, having an abortion?"

"Cynthia Playford wasn't most women," said the gynaecologist testily.

"When was the last time you saw one another, sir?"

"Approximately two months ago. Just before she went in for the abortion. We agreed then not to meet again until after my wife had passed on; and then if we still felt the same way about each other, we'd take things from there, start afresh."

"And Miss Playford, you say, was quite agreeable to this?"

Beamish hesitated. "Ultimately, yes. Naturally, it was a difficult time for her—" he shrugged a little "—more difficult than I had perhaps imagined. I felt that in time she would come round to my way of thinking and see reason, and that if she were only patient everything would come out right in the end and be the same as before, only better, if you understand what I mean."

"Does that mean you felt Miss Playford was in some way being unreasonable?"

They had reached the car park and paused at a red Renault. Beamish put his golf bag in the boot of the car, then walked round to the front of the car and stood with a hand on the door handle ready to get in.

"You'll appreciate that our last meeting was a highly emotional one, Sergeant," he replied. "Miss Playford was under considerable stress, was not herself."

"Did she threaten to take her life?"

Beamish hesitated again. "She made one or two wild threats in that vein. I didn't take them seriously."

"When was this, sir? At your last meeting?"

"No, some weeks later. She rang me two or three times at my Harley Street clinic."

"May I ask why, sir?"

Beamish shrugged. "She knew it was useless to try and get me to change my mind and start seeing her again while my wife was still alive. Then—" he paused, thought for a moment "—the last time she phoned she told me it was all over between us, and I said it was probably for the best. She was becoming very tiresome."

"When was this phone call, sir?"

"Last Thursday, I regret to say. At my clinic. Somewhere around five in the afternoon. She said she was ringing to say good-bye, she wasn't going to sit about twiddling her thumbs—something along those lines—any longer waiting for me to get my life sorted out, and that she and her brother were going away for the weekend together to Wales. I believe she said they were going to attend a magicians' convention—her brother's one, a magician (amateur, of course), and she often accompanied him to this sort of function. He's not married, either." He frowned. "I confess that I wasn't particularly sympathetic towards her. It was getting late and I still had a number of patients waiting to see me. I had hoped to get away early for the holiday weekend. I'm afraid I lost patience with her and terminated our conversation rather abruptly—she was, as I've said, becoming extremely tiresome. It never entered my head that she might be coming close to a complete nervous breakdown. The signs were there, definitely; but then again, she was a very tough lady, physically and emotionally."

"We've all got our breaking point, sir," said the sergeant soberly.

"Yes," said Beamish dryly. He opened the car door; paused. "How did it happen?"

"She fell from the Plaid-yro-Wyth cabin lift into a small graveyard in the valley below. She was impaled on the spiked railings around a grave."

Beamish winced slightly. "If only she'd been patient for just a little while longer. It would've all worked out in the finish. I simply couldn't make her see it." He shook his head and his voice became thoughtful. "It's hard to believe. I'd never have said she was the suicide type, but then—" he sighed "—I'm not a psychiatrist, am I?"

"I'm very sorry if I've misled you, sir," said Rhys-Williams pleasantly. "Miss Playford didn't commit suicide. She was murdered. There was someone—a man—with her when she fell."

Beamish stared at him.

"I wonder, sir," Rhys-Williams went on, reaching into his pocket for his notebook, "if you would mind telling me what you were doing between nine-thirty and ten-thirty yesterday morning?"

CHAPTER 12

"Miss?" Walsh smiled sympathetically at the extremely pretty young woman who had just entered the Marlborough Room. She looked petrified.

She glanced quickly at Sayer before responding. "Sandy . . . I mean, Sandra Coxall."

Walsh smiled again. "Sit down, Miss Coxall." He waved an arm casually in the air. "This won't take but a minute. There are just one or two things I'd like to go over with you."

He opened the file on his desk and removed the statement she had made the previous day. It was short, sweet, and to the point. She had been on duty in reception at approximately eleven-fifteen on Good Friday evening, working later than usual and on overtime because of the magicians' convention, when Miss Cynthia Playford had rung down to the switchboard from her room and requested that Mr. Frank Sexton should be summoned to the telephone to speak with her. The night porter was not available and so, on Miss Playford's insistence, the receptionist herself had gone to the Wellington Room, where the conventioneers were holding a party, to summon Mr. Sexton. She found him there, relayed Miss Playford's message, and together they returned to reception. The receptionist then left him speaking on the telephone at the reception desk while she went to find the night porter to attend to the needs of another guest. When she returned some minutes later, Sexton had gone. It was not until late the following day that she learned that Sexton was hotly denying that he had spoken to Cynthia Playford on the telephone the previous night and claiming that the line had gone dead by the time he had got there.

The young woman shifted nervously on her chair. She was fair, not quite but almost white-haired, with perfect doll-like features and large, dark blue eyes which dominated her face and made it appear even more doll-like. She was wearing a chocolate brown skirt with a brown, beige, and cream plaid waistcoat over a long-sleeved cream silk blouse tied in a voluminous bow at her throat. "Is something wrong?" she ventured timidly. "With my statement, I mean?"

"No—" Walsh looked up and smiled at her. "This is fine."

She relaxed a little, crossing her slim legs neatly and displaying an exceedingly attractive ankle which both men savoured nostalgically.

Walsh went on, "I just wonder, though, Miss . . . er, Coxall—?"

"Sandy," she corrected him with a shy smile. "Everybody calls me that. 'Miss Coxall' makes me feel as though I've suddenly become my father's maiden aunt! And believe me, that's not a nice way for anyone to feel."

He smiled. "Well, then, Sandy. About Miss Playford. What frame of mind would you say she was in when she rang down on Friday night wanting to talk to . . . er—" he consulted her statement "—Mr. Sexton?"

Sandy wrinkled her slightly upturned nose. "That maiden aunt I mentioned—? A lot like her when she can't get her own way about something. She was in quite a state. Very sarcastic. She was that sort, though," she explained seriously. "Never missed a chance to be sarcastic and rude. She was very cutting to some of the other staff, particularly to one or two of the waitresses in the dining room. One of the girls was actually in tears—"

"Tell me," said Walsh, nodding, "what she said to you when she rang down. As best you can remember, of course."

The girl sighed. "Well, very little really. Just that she wanted to talk to Mr. Sexton—oh, and that she'd wait. I told her I'd get Mr. Sexton to call her back because it would probably take me a while to find him, but she wouldn't have it; so I gave up arguing with her and transferred the call from the switchboard to the extension phone on the desk and then went off in search of him. He was in the Wellington Room with his wife and Miss Playford's brother and a few of the other magicians who are here for the convention. I gave him her message—" The blue eyes twinkled mischievously under her long white eyelashes. "Well, that is, first I tried to catch his eye . . . I mean, I didn't see why I should be made a party to Miss Playford's nasty little game."

She glanced at Sayer, who only just in the nick of time remembered his manners and diverted his steady gaze from that delectable ankle. Then, looking back at Walsh, she grinned and said, "Just like the maiden aunt, a real stirrer! You've got no idea the trouble she causes at home between my mum and dad. And me, if she can manage that too," she sighed.

"And that was what you felt Miss Playford was up to? That she was deliberately trying to cause trouble between Mr. and Mrs. Sexton?"

Sandy shrugged. "I don't know for sure, of course, but that's the way it seemed to me. It was certainly the impression I got from what—or rather *the way* Miss Playford spoke to me over the phone. Anyway, in the finish I had to go right up to Mr. Sexton with the message. His wife was furious about it. Not with me," she put in quickly. "Because Miss Playford wanted to talk to her husband."

"What about Mr. Sexton? How did he react?"

"He just looked sick, poor man."

"And Mr. Playford? Did he make any comment or react in any way?"

"He just told Mr. Sexton to stay right where he was and to give me a message for Miss Playford to go and take a running jump."

"But Mr. Sexton ignored this advice and accompanied you back to the reception desk?"

"Yes." Sandy nodded and was quiet for a moment. Then, inclining her head a little to one side and studying Walsh thoughtfully, she said slowly, "I knew he would, you know . . . want to talk to her. Just for a very brief moment when I first gave him

Miss Playford's message, there was something in his eyes—" She paused; gazed intently at the slightly sagging, middle-aged face before her, then with the unbridled candour of youth: "You probably wouldn't understand . . . I mean, *remember* what it feels like to be in love with someone and to hang about indoors by the phone for days and nights on end hoping that person will ring you and all the while knowing deep down in your heart of hearts that they won't and that whatever there was between you is over forever, finished."

She sounded so wistful that Walsh forgave her for pointing out to him that in her very young and very beautiful eyes, he was so far over the hill she couldn't see him any more. Not as a man, anyway. As some sexless father figure, maybe. (Well, that was fair enough; she couldn't be much older than his own daughter.) He couldn't imagine anyone's ever having been so cruel as to keep her hanging about by a phone waiting for a call; but someone had, and the hurt was still there—he could see it in her eyes just as she had seen it in Sexton's.

She nodded slowly. "Well, it was like that; only the thing Mr. Sexton had convinced himself was never going to happen, had actually happened. His eyes suddenly came alive." She smiled sadly. "Miss Playford snapped her fingers and—" she shook her head at the folly of the man "—he went running. Then just as we got back to the desk, Captain Belson came up and wanted to know if he could have a plate of sandwiches sent up to his room; and I went off to find the porter. When I came back, Mr. Sexton had disappeared."

"And the other guest—the one wanting sandwiches?"

"Captain Belson? Yes, he was still there. I told him the sandwiches would be up in about ten or fifteen minutes, and he said thank you and went. And that's about it, I'm afraid. I finished up for the night soon after that . . . at eleven-thirty."

Walsh nodded. "Let's just go back for a minute, if we could, to where you returned with Mr. Sexton to the reception desk. You say you heard Mr. Sexton speaking into the phone as you went off to find the porter?"

"Well, I assumed he was talking on the phone . . . to Miss Playford, that is. I think he said something like, 'Hello, Cyn?'—or maybe it was 'Cynthia'; but then—" she frowned prettily "—that doesn't mean there was somebody at the other end of the line, does it? And apparently Miss Playford had got tired of waiting and rung off. It wouldn't surprise me one little bit if she hadn't really wanted to talk to Mr. Sexton in the first place. All she really wanted was for me to deliver a message to him from her in front of his wife."

"Yes," said Walsh quietly. "Well, thank you, Miss—er, Sandy. You've been most helpful."

"Have I?" She thought about it for a moment, then nodded and said, "Good. Right now, I'd better be getting back to the desk or they'll be sending out a search party for me!"

"Oh, just one more thing before you go, er, Sandy. If you wouldn't mind. The porter who was on duty that night—could I have his name, please?"

"Ted—Edward, I suppose—Black." She stood up, squared the chair neatly against the desk, and grinned. "Black by name and black by nature. He comes on duty at seven of an evening."

"Thank you again, Sandy," said Walsh, and both pairs of male eyes followed her gently swaying hips all the way out of the room.

CHAPTER 13

Kath sat before the dressing-table mirror brushing her hair.

Two hundred and twenty-six, two hundred and twenty-seven . . .

Abruptly, Sexton left the edge of the bed where he had been sitting and crossed to the window which looked out onto a light well. A line from the Noël Coward song went through his head *. . . A room with a view was right . . .* Some view!

Two hundred and thirty-one . . .

It was driving him mad. She hadn't stopped since he'd come in.

He heard the brush go down on the dressing table and looked round expecting to see her rise and start getting ready to go down for lunch, though it was getting a bit late for that. He glanced at his watch—nearly two by it (the competition started at three). But she didn't move; she sat there staring back at him in the mirror.

"What's that look for?" he asked sharply.

"You killed her, didn't you, Frank?" she said quietly. Her eyes filled with tears. "Please don't lie to me, not about this. I—I couldn't bear it. I only wish I could make you understand how important this is to me, that you tell me the truth and confide in me. We can fight this thing together, Frank. Let me help you now like you helped me over Lucy. Please don't shut me out."

Sexton looked away, gazed into the light well. "You're being very childish, Kath," he said wearily. "You know that, don't you? I haven't killed anybody, least of all Cynthia Playford."

Kath covered her face with her hands and sobbed quietly into them. "I can't live without you, Frank. You know that. If they take you away from me, I—"

"Nobody's going to take me away from you," he said irritably. "Now stop it! You're making yourself ill."

Kath wept softly for a short while longer; then, dragging her hands down her cheeks to wipe away the tears, she said, "Won't you at least tell me why she wanted to talk to you on the phone on Friday night?"

Sexton's expression soured and his voice hardened. "I've told you, I've told the police—a thousand times, over and over again—I don't know why she wanted to speak to me. She'd rung off by the time I'd got to the phone."

"And you didn't ring her back?"

"For Christ's sake!" Sexton was shouting now. "How many more times do I have to say it?"

The telephone rang, and he strode over to it and snatched up the receiver. "Yes!" he barked. Then, a little subdued: "Oh, yes, right away. The Marlborough Room. . . . Yes, fine. I'll be right down."

He replaced the receiver and looked at his wife. "The big noise from CID wants a word with me."

Kath stiffened. "You won't let us—Nigel and me—down, will you? About your coat? We were only trying to protect you from yourself. Cynthia Playford isn't worth spending the next few years of your life in jail for, Frank. If her own brother can see that and is willing to stick his neck out for you, why can't you?"

Sexton went to the door, paused as if he had suddenly remembered something, then turned slowly back to face her. Very quietly, he said, "I didn't kill her, Kath. But I can see that you might have. Alone or with your pal Nigel's help. Are you sure his motives are as pure as you think?"

Kath called frantically to him to wait, but he was through the door and gone. The *Do Not Disturb* sign looped over the door-knob swung to and fro like a pendulum, *swish-swish-swish-swish*, slower and slower. She watched it until it stopped altogether, then crossed her arms on the dressing table, laid her head on them, and wept bitterly. Then, suddenly, she fell silent; raised her head; stared at herself in the mirror. The clairvoyante. . . . Kath cleared the tears from her eyes, looked quickly at the time, and hastily repaired her makeup. Frank wouldn't approve. She had wanted to consult a clairvoyante once before, soon after Lucy had died, but Frank had said no. Well, this time he wasn't there to say yea or nay. And she had to talk to someone. The worry was driving her out of her mind. . . .

"Mr. Sexton?" Walsh, half rising in his chair, leaned across the desk, shook Sexton by the hand, and motioned him to be seated. "Good of you to spare me the time. I understand you're judging some kind of competition shortly."

"After lunch," said Sexton, drawing out a chair and sitting down. "At three to be precise. Plenty of time."

Walsh regarded him thoughtfully. "You haven't eaten?"

Sexton shrugged off the concern he thought he heard in Walsh's voice. "It's all right. I'm not really hungry; and besides, we're holding our banquet this evening and I usually try to avoid two heavy meals in one day."

Sayer, at his post near the fireplace, ran an experienced eye quickly over Sexton; the sleek, silvery grey silk suit and hand-made maroon leather shoes. Sexton had an air about him, a heady mixture of success and another more elusive ingredient which Sayer couldn't for the moment isolate and identify. He thought it might be the moneyed stench of corruption; in fact he would have bet on it.

"I've decided not to beat about the bush," Sexton announced without further preamble. "You're going to get the story from the others, but I'd rather you heard it first from me. That is, I hope I'm not being naive there . . . in thinking I'm going to be first." He paused, waited for Walsh to say something. Then, with a resigned shrug: "Cynthia Playford and I had an affair."

"Had?"

"Yes. Very much past tense. It was all over between us eighteen months ago. My wife found out what was going on, and

. . . well, I'll come straight to the point—" he shrugged again "—if I don't, someone else will; and as I've said, I'd far rather it came from me. There was a pretty awful scene over it in public between my wife and Miss Playford . . . at one of the magicians' functions we attended together—Miss Playford and her brother, and my wife and I." He smiled wryly. "That's why I'm so sure you're going to hear all about Cynthia Playford and me. I've got my enemies out there—" he inclined his head at the door "—people who'd love a chance to stick the boot in and see me fall flat on my face." He hesitated, looked at Walsh speculatively. "Well, that gives my wife a reason for wanting Miss Playford out of the way, and I daresay you won't think much of me for providing you so readily with a motive."

"It's all really rather academic, Mr. Sexton," said Walsh. "Whether or not your wife had a motive for killing Miss Playford. We aren't looking for a woman in connection with the crime, not unless there's one around who's over six feet tall, going grey at the temples—" he glanced casually at the smudges of silver-grey at either side of Sexton's otherwise dark head "—and who dresses and looks like a man. Not to mention having the strength of one."

The puzzled expression on Sexton's face took a moment to clear. "Oh . . . oh, yes, I see what you mean." He paused and frowned. "It's true, then, what they're saying—that Cynthia was shoved out of one of those cabin things that go up the mountain?"

Walsh ignored the question and went on as though Sexton had not spoken. "However, now that you've brought it up, the affair you say you had with Miss Playford—were you still in love with her?"

Sexton looked him coolly in the eye. Never faltered for a moment. "Yes," he said. "I was in love with her, but she wasn't with me. And while we're about it—confession time and all that!—there's something else I think you should know. The tartan-lined raincoat—"

Walsh made no comment, but waited.

"The one worn by the man everyone's saying was last seen with Miss Playford," Sexton continued in a flat, rather weary voice. "I've got one just like it. . . . It was stolen from that small lounge off reception sometime on Friday."

"Has it been recovered?" asked Walsh.

Sexton hesitated, thoughtfully massaged his jaw between the thumb and second finger of his right hand, then pinched his chin, making a dimple in it with his forefinger. "Well, yes and no. I understand Nigel Playford's got it now. It turned up on one of the coat stands yesterday afternoon and my wife found it—"

Walsh widened his eyes. "And gave it to Mr. Playford?"

There was a long slence. Then Sexton sighed. "My wife has convinced herself that I had something to do with Cynthia Playford's death." His shoulders sagged and he wiped a hand tiredly across his eyes. "As a matter of fact, it's getting to be a bit of a bore. She isn't a well woman, hasn't been for years—not since we lost our only child in a road accident."

Sayer glanced expectantly at Walsh; but the Chief Inspector left Mrs. Sexton's poor state of health and what, in Sexton's opinion, was the cause of it alone and went back to the raincoat. And that, thought Sayer, was another mistake . . . not to encourage someone to expand on what was obviously a mental disorder rather than a physical one.

"You say your raincoat was stolen from the lounge on Good Friday?"

Sexton nodded. "I didn't go straight up to our room on Friday morning after my wife and I had checked in. Somebody—Lance Headley, one of the convention organisers (you've no doubt met him)—waylaid me in reception with some minor problems over today's competition, and I left my wife to go on up alone with the porter and unpack while Mr. Headley and I went into the lounge to iron things out.

"Naturally, having only just come in from the street—the garage out in back of the hotel, actually—I was wearing a raincoat which was pretty well soaked through (it bucketed down seconds after my wife and I'd left the cover of the garage); so I removed it and hung it up on a coat stand to dry. Then I promptly forgot all about it until sometime late in the afternoon when my wife asked me what I'd done with it. I remembered immediately where I'd left it, but when I went downstairs to get it, it'd gone. I did mention it to the hotel staff—" Sexton was suddenly very much on the defensive "—you know, in case they'd shifted it somewhere else for some reason or other; but nobody had seen it. Then sometime after lunch yesterday, my wife spotted it hanging up where I'd said I'd left it; and without saying anything to me about it then, she talked things over with Nigel Playford—by this time she'd heard the rumour about a raincoat, one like mine with a tartan lining; everyone had!—and they decided between themselves that he would pretend it was his."

Walsh looked at him thoughtfully. "Why?" he asked.

Sexton shrugged a little. "I've told you, it only stands to reason—" another shrug "—that the coat everyone was talking about had to be mine. I should've thought it was obvious," he said coolly. "Somebody's out to frame me. What other explanation could there be for its having gone missing for over twenty-four hours and then suddenly turning up again?" He smiled forbiddingly. "Added to which, of course, is the little matter of my alibi—"

Walsh turned up the file on the desk, glanced at somethng in there, then nodded.

"Well?" demanded Sexton.

"Well *what*, Mr. Sexton?"

"I haven't an alibi for the crucial period of time yesterday morning."

"Oh, yes," said Walsh slowly. He nodded again. "You don't think anybody saw you on the beach—" the Chief Inspector was referring to something in the file again "—that was it, wasn't it? You left the hotel around nine and went for a walk alone along the seafront . . . beach," he corrected himself, "and didn't return to the hotel until shortly before eleven. Without a topcoat? Rather chilly I would've thought, but never mind—" he looked up "—we won't go into that for the moment."

He closed the file and leaned back in his chair and considered Sexton in silence for a moment or two. "So your wife and Mr. Playford thought they would rectify your problem over your look-alike raincoat by Mr. Playford pretending it was his."

"That seems to have been the general idea. Playford had an alibi; I didn't."

"Mr. Playford is a particular frend of yours?"

"I wouldn't say 'particular.' A friend, yes. We've known each other for a good many years. All of us had—known each other for a long time—that is, the Playfords (Cynthia and Nigel) and my wife and myself."

"What exactly were your feelings when Miss Playford decided she was no longer in love with you and wished to terminate your affair—what, eighteen months ago, you said?"

"Thereabouts. Cynthia didn't end it. It was my wife who did the terminating. She threatened to—" Sexton didn't finish, and Walsh made no attempt to press him to continue. After a short pause, Sexton went on, "It wasn't what I wanted. I was prepared to ask Kath, my wife, for a divorce; but it seemed—" he laughed bitterly "—well, it was almost as though the moment Kath showed her claws, Cynthia lost interest."

"Your wife's threat disturbed her?"

Sexton was in no hurry to answer. He sat in silence for some moments, then frowned and said, "It took me a long time to figure it out, just what it was that Cynthia was really up to, but I finally came to the conclusion that it was never me; it was my wife who interested Cynthia—how far she could push her over our affair before she'd do something about it. And the moment Cynthia had got her answer, that was it, she had no further use for me, though occasionally—" he smiled grimly "—Cynthia couldn't resist twisting the knife, using me, of course, to do it." He shook his head. "She was one very strange lady. As mixed up as hell. And anyway—" He broke off, frowning.

"Yes?" Walsh prompted him.

"It was nothing . . . just something Cynthia once said to me about her brother. I thought she was joking, but now I'm not so sure about that." He hesitated, shifted in his seat, then gazed at his hands which were splayed out, palms down, over his knees. "I loathe gutter talk, but—" he sighed "—what people have always whispered about Playford and his sister was, I think, basically true. I couldn't see it at the time, but Cynthia more or less admitted it to me herself when I told her I'd get a divorce and we'd marry. She laughed and said she'd no intention of ever getting married, and when I asked why not, she said because she'd never found anyone the equal of her brother. Nor, she said, did she ever expect to." He looked up and smiled a little. "Make what you like of that."

Whatever Walsh made of it was his secret. The room was quiet with Sexton's unspoken regret at what might have been. Then Walsh said, "If we could come now to last Friday night and the call Miss Playford made from her room to the switchboard requesting that you should be summoned to the phone to speak to her. . . ."

Sexton nodded. Then, when Walsh remained silent and it became clear to him that he was expected to say something: "There's nothing really to tell. The receptionist came into the Wellington Room—this would've been somewhere about a quarter past eleven—and told me that Miss Playford wanted to speak to me on the telephone. At first I didn't understand what she meant; I thought Cynthia must've gone off somewhere—left the hotel—and was phoning me from outside. Playford thought so too and queried the girl about it; but she said no, Miss Playford was ringing down from her room. So I got up and went with her out to the phone on the reception desk."

"Your wife raised no objection to this?"

"Quite frankly, I can't remember. I didn't really pay much attention to her. It'd come as a bit of a shock—well, in a way it had. Cynthia was notorious for stirring up trouble; but then she and Kath seemed to have patched things up between them—you know, the way some women do, the wife and the mistress ganging up together against the poor defenceless male—so I couldn't quite make it out. What could be so urgent that Cynthia had to talk to me like that instead of just simply coming back down-stairs and having a quiet word with me; or even waiting and see-ing me at breakfast next morning? Playford might've known what it was all about; I don't know. I remember he was pretty quick to say I should let Cynthia stew in her own juice, or words to that effect."

Walsh interrupted. "He didn't actually say, though, that he knew why his sister wanted to talk to you?"

"No, he just advised me not to go to the phone. It's since then that I've wondered if perhaps he knew why she wanted to speak to me. Anyway, I got up and went to the phone, but by this time Cynthia had rung off. The line was dead."

"Did you try to get her back?"

"No. The receptionist had gone off somewhere looking for the night porter to get sandwiches, or something of the sort, for one of the other guests; and there was no one else on the desk to put me through on the switchboard. So I went straight back to the Wellington Room."

"You didn't think to go up to her room and speak to her face to face?"

"No," said Sexton. He shook his head. "That would've really been asking for trouble. With my wife, I mean. . . ."

CHAPTER 14

It was much as Mrs. Charles had expected. Ada Toomey's main interest in the future lay entirely with her concern for her husband's well-being; and when she rose to leave, she did so reassured and happy with the reading the clairvoyante had given her.

Mrs. Belson, whom Mrs. Charles saw next—a reserved, dignified woman who did not have Mrs. Toomey's more outgoing, uninhibited personality—was much less forthcoming and direct in the phrasing of the questions which she laid before the clairvoyante. But they amounted to much the same thing, though something about her manner over and above her natural reserve and self-composure suggested that she already knew what the future held in store for her insofar as her husband was concerned. Mrs. Toomey had glanced interestedly at the crystal ball centred on the small table at which she and the clairvoyante had been seated, but had asked specifically for a reading of the Tarot. Mrs. Belson ignored the crystal completely, which had been moved aside while the clairvoyante had read the Tarot for Mrs. Toomey, and proffered, without a word, the palm of her right hand for the clairvoyante to read.

From the moment she sat down and held out her hand, the impression conveyed by Mrs. Belson to the clairvoyante was that she should not be told anything she did not specifically desire to hear. Mrs. Charles respected her unspoken wish and remained silent, waiting for Mrs. Belson to offer her questions in her own time and in her own way. Mrs. Toomey and Mrs. Belson were classic examples of the two types of client who generally consulted the clairvoyante: those like Mrs. Toomey, garrulous and excitable, who went for the direct, no-holds-barred approach; and those like Mrs. Belson who chose the long way round to ask what, in Mrs. Toomey's and Mrs. Belson's case, was basically the same question.

Mrs. Belson began by saying she was extremely worried about her husband's proposal that they should sell up and retire to Malta where they had spent some time early in their marriage and had been extremely happy.

Mrs. Charles gazed at Mrs. Belson's palm. She did not look up when she spoke. "You are afraid that you will both regret the move and not be happy out there?"

"Oh no," said Mrs. Belson quickly. "It's not that. I know we'll be happy there. We both love the place. It's—" She hesitated, but the clairvoyante deliberately didn't look up, but kept her gaze fixed on the palm held before her—the strong lifeline; the many long years Mrs. Belson would spend alone, a widow. "It's just that," Mrs. Belson continued, finally facing up to her fear, as the clairvoyante had already foreseen, that she might very soon be on her own, "I'm afraid it wouldn't be a very wise thing to do." She hesitated again. "You see, all our friends are here—we don't really know anybody at all in Malta, not now; and if . . . well, if something were to happen to either one of us—"

The clairvoyante looked up slowly as Mrs. Belson faltered. The expression in the latter's eyes saddened. "I must try and talk James out of it, mustn't I?" she said quietly.

Mrs. Belson withdrew her hand, curling it into a loose fist, signalling her desire to terminate the reading at this point.

The clairvoyante smiled at her kindly and said softly, "In your hand I saw that you and your husband have had many happy years together, a marriage that has been far happier than most. Let that thought and that thought alone sustain you now and in the days ahead."

As Mrs. Belson rose, Mrs. Charles's lowered gaze came to rest on the crystal which she had been about to replace in the centre of the table. Mrs. Belson, who had been on the point of thanking the clairvoyante for seeing her, watched the colour drain from her face. "What is it?" she demanded sharply.

There was a slight noise in the doorway, an abrupt "Sorry!" and the clairvoyante and Mrs. Belson looked quickly at the woman who had unintentionally intruded on them. It was Kath Sexton. She turned away, but Mrs. Belson called her back. "It's all right, Mrs. Sexton," she said. "You can come in. I was just leaving."

"The door wasn't closed," said Kath defensively, moving forward hesitantly. She shrugged apologetically at the clairvoyante. "I naturally thought you were free."

Mrs. Belson thanked the clairvoyante; then, giving Kath a quick smile, she left. After a moment's indecision, Kath took Mrs. Belson's place at the table with the clairvoyante.

"Were you waiting long?" inquired Mrs. Charles.

Kath assumed that this was the clairvoyante's way of asking whether she had been eavesdroppng on her conversation with Mrs. Belson. "Only a few seconds," said Kath. "I couldn't hear what you were saying."

"Are you quite sure it was for only a few seconds?" asked the clairvoyante.

Kath frowned. For God's sake, what was this? The Spanish Inquisition? "Well, maybe for a bit longer than that," she admitted irritably. "A minute or so. But it doesn't make any difference. I still didn't hear what you were saying." Her features, which were already pinched and drawn, became bitter and hard. "You were talking about me and Frank, weren't you?"

"No," replied the clairvoyante. "Mrs. Belson and I were discussing neither you nor your husband."

"So?" said Kath, a trifle defiantly. "Why all the fuss about how long I was standing there watching you?"

"I saw something in the crystal, Mrs. Sexton," said the clairvoyante imperturbably. "I think at the precise instant that you perhaps entered the room. This, and this alone—the exact moment you entered the room—was all I wished to establish."

"Why should that be so important?" Kath's eyes narrowed

accusingly. "You saw something in the crystal about me, didn't you?"

"Not necessarily, Mrs. Sexton," the clairvoyante replied—evasively, Kath chose to think. "There were three people in the room. The special significance of what I saw in the crystal a few moments ago—and I stress that it need not necessarily be of *special* significance—could have applied to any one of us."

Kath eyed her disbelievingly. "Why should you be affected by what you saw?"

"It was my mother's face," said the clairvoyante simply.

Kath stared at her. "What on earth would seeing your mother's face have to do with me?"

"I have no idea, Mrs. Sexton," said the clairvoyante. "Not without going further into it."

"You mean you'd have to look at the crystal ball again . . . now?"

Mrs. Charles hesitated. Kath Sexton was the one person whom she had hoped would not consult her for a private reading. Cynthia Playford had never mentioned her affair with Frank Sexton to her; it was something the clairvoyante had learnt about only that weekend. And from the gossip and rumours currently circulating about the Sextons, particularly those concerning Mrs. Sexton's present emotional state, Mrs. Charles feared the consequences of any reading given her, certainly one given in these highly emotional circumstances. She knew Kath would be adamant; no one now could dissuade her from having her fortune told, but the clairvoyante felt obliged to try.

She spoke very quietly. "Please think about this very carefully, Mrs. Sexton. Are you quite sure you really want me to look in the crystal for you?"

Kath stuck out her chin; the look of defiance was back in her eye again. "If there's something bad there, then I want to know what it is. I'm sick and tired of putting my head in the sand. That's what it boils down to, you know. That's the advice everyone—including my husband—has been giving me for years. Pretend. *Pretend* it hasn't happened, Kath. *Forget* it, Kath." Her mouth set in a hard, straight line; the look she gave the clairvoyante was ice-cold. "*No.* I can't pretend any more; I *won't* pretend any more! I'm not a child. I want the truth and I want it now!"

Mrs. Charles looked at her for a very long moment, then lowered her gaze to the crystal.

"Well?" demanded Kath when the seconds lengthened into what seemed like the longest minute of her entire life.

"I see a man," said the clairvoyante distantly. "A man running. . . ."

"My husband?" asked Kath quickly, defiance leaving her voice and being replaced by childlike anxiety.

The clairvoyante raised her eyes. "I cannot tell. His face is in shadow. But he is very frightened, in terrible danger."

"What is this man running away from—the police?"

The clairvoyante looked down again. Then, mercifully, the crystal clouded over. The vision, the vividly clear picture of a man running—not from the police but, inexplicably in the circumstances, from the woman awaiting the clairvoyante's response—faded.

"I'm sorry, Mrs. Sexton," said the clairvoyante. "The crystal has clouded. I can tell you no more for now."

"You mean you won't!" snapped Kath. She got up angrily. "Well, thank you very much. I am sorry to have taken up so much of your valuable time."

She stormed out of the room, ignoring the clairvoyante's call for her to wait.

Mrs. Charles sighed as Kath slammed the door behind her. She had handled that badly; but she doubted that it would be any different, even if she were given the opportunity to wipe out that disastrous beginning and start all over again with the woman. In Kath Sexton she could see Cynthia Playford. Kath Sexton had reached the same high, an emotional peak where only a miracle now could save her from destroying herself and those around her.

Mrs. Charles closed her eyes, recalled those few seconds before Kath had made her presence known.

Why had she seen her mother's face in the crystal? What was the connection between her mother and Kath Sexton? Or was it something else, some warning her mother was trying to give her concerning the woman?

The clairvoyante's thoughts moved on to the second vision. A man running. . . . Logically, or so it seemed for the moment, that man was Frank Sexton. But why was he running away from his wife; why was that part of the vision so alarmingly clear? And to whom did the danger really apply? She had elected to tell Kath that it was the man who was in danger; but the truth of the matter was that this was debatable. The danger could apply equally well to the other person in the vision, to Kath. And if so, then the reason why the man was running away from her was because he had killed her.

One of them—either Kath Sexton, *probably* Kath Sexton, or the man—was definitely marked down for death.

CHAPTER 15

A pint of beer in each hand, Sayer waited outside the ballroom for Walsh to join him. Walsh had said he wouldn't be long. Nigel Playford had reported an envelope missing from his sister's shoulder bag when asked to identify it and its contents, and Walsh wanted to check her hotel room himself in case the missing envelope was there and had somehow been overlooked by Rhys-Williams when he had gone through her other belongings the previous day.

Sayer glanced in at the ballroom door but couldn't see a thing. The ballroom had been subdivided with a thick yellow curtain, and the stage and the audience were beyond it out of sight. Then he heard voices in the corridor leading into the one in which he was waiting, and he assumed that Walsh was finally on his way.

It turned out to be an elderly couple, the man in a loud check suit, the woman less flamboyantly dressed in a pale wool trouser-suit somewhat after the shade of her wispy, apricot-coloured hair.

Their manner was positively furtive. They were definitely up to something. Sayer knew the look; only he was more accustomed to seeing it on much younger people, kids. They had hesitated on turning the corner and seeing him standing outside the ballroom, both pausing guiltily. And then, without a word or sign passing between them, they fixed their gaze on some spot in the far distance—they were so convincing about it that even Sayer's eyes were drawn that way to see if there was someone or something interesting there—and walked straight past with not so much as a sidelong glance at him, disappearing at length around another corner.

Sayer smiled to himself. They would be back. There was nothing down there but a dusty, unlit cloakroom (not in use). *Maybe they were pinching the wire coat hangers!* A minute passed and then back they came. Quite nonchalantly, in the circumstances.

Sayer hazarded a guess as they neared him. "The magic competition?" He indicated his head over his shoulder. "It's being held in there."

"It's all right, is it?" the man asked doubtfully. "We can go in?" He suddenly came clean. "We're not with the convention people, you know."

"Neither am I," Sayer confided.

"Yes, but that's different," said the man. "You're something to do with the police, aren't you? Investigating the Playford woman's death. You can go where you like; nobody's going to stop you, are they? We're just ordinary hotel guests. Toomey's the name." He didn't bother to offer his hand: Sayer, who was still clutching the beers, was in no position to take anything that was offered to him. "This is the wife," Toomey added as an afterthought, and Mrs. Toomey and Sayer exchanged nods.

There was some laughter inside the ballroom and a short burst of applause. Toomey's face fell. "It's started, has it?"

"Yes, but only just: that's the first act. You haven't missed much of the show."

"Not the girl, I hope?" said Toomey quickly. He didn't bother to say which girl; took it for granted that Sayer had red blood in his veins and would therefore know very well whom he meant. Toomey frowned. "I don't suppose it'll hurt if the missus and I sneak in and stand up at the back, out of everyone's way. They can only throw us out, can't they?"

There was another, longer round of applause, and Sayer glanced in. "I'd wait a minute if I were you until the lights go down again and the next act goes on."

"You're going in, are you?" asked Toomey.

"In a minute. I'm waiting for someone."

Toomey turned to his wife. "Perhaps we should wait for a bit and go in with the police and then nobody'll take any notice of us."

He looked back at Sayer. "The girl's on third. You're sure that's only the first act?"

Sayer nodded. "She sounds special," he observed.

"You can say that again," said Toomey with a nod and a wink. "I didn't think she'd make it," he added. "Not after what happened between her and Miss Playford's brother at the party on Friday night. She really rubbed Miss Playford up the wrong way. She was one of the judges, you know . . . Miss Playford, that is. They've had to get someone else to take her place."

"There was some trouble, was there?" Sayer asked conversationally. "At the party you mentioned?"

"Well, not so much *at* the party, though that was when it all began. The girl—the one in the competition—made her big play for Mr. Playford . . . He's a judge too, by the way. It was afterwards, after the Playfords left the party—"

Sayer interrupted. "Miss Playford and her brother left the party together—Miss Playford didn't leave on her own?"

"No," said Mrs. Toomey. "They both went off together soon after the girl had played up to Mr. Playford." She looked at her husband. "Just before eleven, wasn't it? I remember that because it was at eleven that we decided to call it a night; and when we got up to our floor, the two of them were standing outside Miss Playford's room having a right old dingdong of a row about the way the girl had carried on with Mr. Playford on the dance floor. Miss Playford was furious with her brother about it. Then she went into her room and slammed the door; and after a bit he turned around—he followed us for a while along the corridor as if he was going to his room—and then he went back downstairs again to the party. That's the way it looked to my husband, anyway. I didn't see what he did; my husband was the one watching to see what he was going to do."

"Did you hear what the Playfords said to one another?"

"No, not really. But we knew what it was all about, didn't

we?" Mrs. Toomey said to her husband. "Just as well for the girl, I'd say, that Miss Playford isn't going to be one of the judges this afternoon after all. She'd never have got her vote."

There was some more applause, and Toomey started forward anxiously and peered round the door, but the houselights remained down.

"I'd go on in if I were you," Sayer advised them. "We could be some while yet."

In the event, it was halfway through Alison Crosby's act that Walsh and Sayer slipped quietly through the yellow dividing curtain, excusing themselves as they passed in front of the Toomeys and moved on to stand unobtrusively at the back.

Sayer supposed the girl was a good magician; that was not one of the things he noticed about her. She was wearing one of the briefest costumes he had ever seen, covered in pale blue sequins and cut way up her thighs, almost to her waist it seemed to him, and split way down the centre-front almost to her navel. The blaring taped music to which she performed was from *Saturday Night Fever*. So was the choreography which linked her magic act and maintained her voluptuous body in perpetual sensuous motion.

"No wonder Miss Playford was a little upset," he murmured. He leaned towards Walsh and briefed him quickly and quietly about the Playfords' argument over the girl's advances to Nigel Playford at the Night-Before Party. Walsh listened, nodded, but made no comment. Then the lights came up and the audience applauded enthusiastically. One or two of the younger men forgot themselves and whistled shrilly (this was essentially a family weekend and lewdness was frowned upon), and the girl smiled coyly, dipped daintily at the knee, waved, then skipped offstage into the wings.

"Shall we?" Walsh suggested, inclining his head at the doorway.

Sayer nodded, deposited their empty beer glasses with some others on a glass mosaic pillar-surround, and then they moved quietly towards the exit (the Toomeys, Sayer noted, had sneaked forward under cover of darkness into two unoccupied seats near the back).

Walsh and Sayer made their way in silence along a confusing network of corridors to the Marlborough Room. They went in. Walsh closed the door, then crossed to the desk and sat down. Sayer, drawing up a chair, said, "Find anything interesting in Cynthia Playford's room?"

Walsh shook his head. "Her brother's creating quite a fuss about this envelope he insists has gone missing; wants us to get up a search party and go over every square inch of the valley she nose-dived into; but I personally reckon the goat got it." He broke off to explain about the billy goat with the bizarre appetite for red woollen scarves and ladies' footwear which had caused the police so much trouble during their initial search of the valley. He went on, "Her shoulder bag fell open during her fall and everything in it was scattered over a fairly wide area. However, according to Playford, we recovered everything but the envelope."

"What was in it?"

"Playford hasn't the vaguest idea. But he swears it was in her bag—certainly on Friday when they were driving here. She went to her bag at one stage and he spotted it in there, wedged, he says, between her money wallet and her appointment diary."

Sayer's eyebrows rose. "A diary?" Then, after a slight pause: "Anything interesting there?"

Walsh shook his head. "I doubt it. I haven't really had time to examine it closely." He hesitated and looked keenly at Sayer. "Something's bothering you, isn't it? What's on your mind?"

There were a number of things bothering Sayer, not the least of which was Cynthia Playford's appointment diary and Walsh's somewhat cavalier attitude towards it. But he decided to leave it for the moment. Although Walsh's head cold appeared to be drying up, possibly due to his having taken some medication for this purpose, he did not look at all well; and this, Sayer was prepared to admit, was probably contributing heavily towards Walsh's rather listless (in his opinion) handling of the case.

"Sexton," said Sayer at length. "He's lying. He talked to Cynthia Playford late on Friday night. Ask yourself. . . . Sexton's nursing a white-hot passion for the woman—someone who's tossed him aside and said she doesn't want to know any more—and then suddenly she snaps her fingers and he, not surprisingly in the circumstances, goes running, tongue hanging out (and it's on this point, the fact that he did go running when she snapped her pinkies at him that I'm basing my whole argument); he gets to the phone and then the world collapses about him. The love of his life has gone; hung up. Only she's not gone, not really. She's just a short lift ride away."

Sayer folded his arms and leaned back in his chair. "I think he was telling the truth about the phone, that she'd rung off by the time he'd got there; and we know he was telling the truth about the receptionist, that with her off somewhere playing hunt-the-night-porter there was no one at the desk to reconnect him with Cynthia Playford. But as for the rest of it. . . ." He shook his head. "Lying through his teeth. Sexton wouldn't have left it at that; he'd have had to find out what she'd wanted him for. So one way or another, he's lying. Either he talked to her on the phone—she was still there hanging on—or he was telling the truth about that—she'd rung off—and he went up to her room."

"The other guest should know one way or the other—the one waiting at the reception desk wanting a late-night snack."

"That's what I've been thinking. The receptionist said he came up just as she and Sexton got to the desk, and she also said he hung about out there until she returned from her search for the porter, so he must've overheard Sexton's conversation; or if there was no proper conversation as such, must've seen which direction Sexton took off in when he put the phone down—whether he went straight back to the party as he claimed, or whether he headed for the lift or the stairs."

Walsh nodded thoughtfully, then leaned forward and picked up the telephone receiver. "Let's find out, shall we?"

CHAPTER 16

It might have been a trick of the light, the grey, shadowy way it lay across his broad cheekbones, but Captain Belson did not look a well man to Sayer. Far from it. His breathlessness when speaking at length was today noticeably pronounced, so much so that Sayer was conscious of every breath the man drew and was put uncomfortably in mind of a particularly harrowing television programme he had watched recently linking cigarette smoking with lung cancer. He hoped though that he was mistaken in what he was thinking and that Belson was at worst an asthmatic.

Mrs. Belson, Sayer suspected, shared his concern for her husband's health. She didn't want to make a nuisance of herself, she had said with a too bright smile as she had preceded her husband into the Marlborough Room, but she hoped the Chief Inspector didn't mind her coming along too; they were going out for a stroll around the town as soon as her husband was through here, and in the meanwhile she would be at something of a loose end. . . .

Walsh, who had himself already guessed that Belson might be gravely ill and could hear the underlying anxiety in her voice, had hastened to assure her that it was perfectly all right, just routine, and that there was no reason at all why she shouldn't be present and hear what he had to say to her husband. He only wished to clear up one or two small points concerning a telephone conversation which he understood Captain Belson might have overheard.

With a quick nod of his head, Belson endorsed his wife's assurance that they were only too willing to help the police with their inquiries into the tragic death of poor Miss Playford. But what phone call would that have been?

Walsh referred briefly to the file on the desk; then, with a friendly but tired smile at Belson, he said, "I believe you were in the vicinity of the reception desk sometime soon after eleven on Friday night."

Belson nodded and wheezed a little. "Yes, Chief Inspector. My wife and I had spent the evening in the Wellington Room. There was a bit of a party going on in there—all part and parcel of the magic convention that's being held here in the hotel this weekend." He paused to catch his breath. "It was all very friendly and informal, and as the evening wore on everybody joined in the fun. We went up to our room shortly before eleven, then my wife said she felt a little peckish, so I came back down again to see if I could get the night porter to rustle up some sandwiches for her."

With a small, apologetic smile for the delay, Belson paused again to regularise his breathing. "I'd tried phoning down to the desk," he explained after a moment or two, "but there was no answer. I thought the receptionist—or whoever was supposed to be keeping an eye on the switchboard—had probably slipped away to the Wellington Room for a few minutes while it was quiet to have a look at the magic, so I decided I'd probably save time and my temper—" he smiled "—if I were to come down in person and get things organised."

Belson was pausing now more frequently to refill his lungs and speaking slower and more jerkily.

He continued, "Then as I crossed from the lift to the reception desk, as you said, at a little after eleven—about ten or a quarter past, I would've said (though I didn't look at the time)—I could see immediately why nobody was answering the switchboard. The receptionist had gone off to the Wellington Room to fetch one of the other guests to the phone—Mr. Sexton (we were introduced to him and his wife earlier in the evening by Mr. Headley, the president of the club, who was responsible for this weekend's magic *eisteddfod*)—" he grinned at his little joke "—and she and

Mr. Sexton were just making their way back. Mr. Sexton walked up to the phone on the desk (I'd noticed by this time that the receiver was off); and I asked the young lady about some sandwiches."

"What happened then?"

"She went off to the kitchen, I think, to see to it."

"No," said Walsh, shaking his head. "I meant about Mr. Sexton. What was he doing all this while? Was he still talking on the phone?"

Belson shook his head regretfully. "I don't really know what happened there. I can't say I paid all that much attention to him; I was more concerned to see to it that the girl didn't do one of those disappearing acts that hotel staff are so clever at."

Walsh smiled faintly. "Can you remember whether he said anything at all?"

Belson frowned. "I'm sorry but I'm not really sure. My impression is that he did say something, 'hello,' I think—" the frown deepened "—or perhaps it was just simply 'yes'. You know, the way people say 'yes' with a question mark in their voices when they pick up the phone and answer it." He struggled for a moment to get his breath. Then, continuing: "I'm awfully sorry I can't be more helpful; but . . . well, frankly, I wasn't the least bit interested in what he was doing; there was no reason why I should've been. I can see him there in my mind's eye, leaning a little against the desk—" Belson had closed his eyes as an *aide-mémoire* "—the receiver was in his hand. . . ."

Walsh interrupted. "What about his facial expression? Did that register with you?"

Belson looked at him and shook his head apologetically. "No, sorry. I didn't look that closely at him. Then he replaced the receiver and went whizzing off past me to catch the lift. I had to wait for it to come back down again."

Walsh made no comment and looked casually at Sayer, who displayed no reaction whatsoever to Belson's confirmation of the worthlessness of Sexton's testimony. Walsh looked back at Belson and nodded; then thought for a moment. "Your room is on which floor, Captain?"

"The second."

"You went straight up to your room when the lift came back down again for you?"

"Yes, of course," replied Belson, puzzled.

"Did you hear anything, raised voices perhaps, or see any-one—" Walsh's eyebrows shot up "—Mr. Sexton, Miss Playford?—when you got out of the lift at the second floor and walked back along the corridor to your room?"

Belson shook his head very slowly. "No, not a living soul," he replied breathlessly. "The corridor was deserted except for my-self. There wasn't a peep from anyone."

Walsh nodded again and turned to Mrs. Belson. "What about you, Mrs. Belson? Did you hear anything unusual—the sound of people arguing, say—while you were waiting for your husband to return?"

"No," she said. "I'm sorry but I didn't hear anything, either. It was particularly quiet up there. Most people, I think, were still at the party. And our room—" She hesitated, looked embarrassed. Then, with an apologetic smile: "I was going to say that our room is at the opposite end of the corridor to Miss Playford's—quite some distance away—but that would've been presump-tuous, wouldn't it? You didn't say that this was where there might've been an argument taking place, did you?"

Walsh smiled a little and said, "Thank you both; you've been most helpful. I doubt if I'll need to trouble you again." He rose, still smiling. "I hope you enjoy the rest of your holiday here."

"Second honeymoon," Mrs. Belson corrected him with a shy smile as she and her husband also got to their feet. "I was a war bride. We honeymooned here during the first few weeks of the Second World War—just for one very brief day, that's all the time we had together before my husband had to rejoin his ship. We've been promising ourselves for years that we'd come back one of these days and finish what we started, but you know how it is," she sighed. "Time slips by so quickly; and there was always something else to do, some other place we wanted specifically to see." She smiled fondly at her husband, and Walsh wasn't mistaken in thinking that her eyes were suddenly abnormally moist.

He thanked them again and they shook hands; then he went with them as far as the door. As he reached out to open it for them, Mrs. Belson said, "I feel dreadfully sorry for Mr. Sexton. He loved her, you know . . . Miss Playford. I was watching him—" she smiled wistfully "—watching her at the party on Friday night, and you could see it in his eyes. I hate to think what that poor man must be going through. . . ."

Walsh, on drawing open the door, found himself gazing directly into the dark eyes of the intense-looking, middle-aged woman who had been about to knock and enter the room. He could tell by the look on her face that she had heard what Mrs. Belson had said about Sexton. And there could be no mistaking who the woman was.

Kath Sexton stared hard at Walsh for a moment longer, then mumbled, "Sorry, wrong room," swung about abruptly on her heel, and walked quickly away.

There was a breathless hush. Mrs. Belson looked sick. "Oh, my God," she murmured. "That poor woman. She heard. I'd better go after her and apologise. No, you James—you're better at handling these things than I am. You go after her."

"What?" he said blankly. Those few steps behind his wife and Walsh, he wasn't too sure what was going on. Then, gazing along the corridor after Kath Sexton, he said, "Oh, yes. Bad show." He frowned. "Yes, leave it with me, my dear; I'll have a word with her."

Walsh returned to the desk, frowning over what had happened, and sat down. Glancing at the time, he picked up the telephone receiver and said, "I think I'll see if I can track down this night-porter chappie—Ted-whatever-his-name-is. Black, Ted Black. He should be clocking in about now. Let's see if any interesting developments were taking place up on the second floor when he delivered Mrs. Belson's sandwiches."

Ted Black, who was probably in his early fifties, was a diminutive man—just under five feet tall so not really a dwarf, though there was something of that look about him. A spinal injury, the result of a fall from his cot when a baby, had given him badly rounded shoulders. He liked to tell people that he had got the back injury during his teens after falling from a horse. He looked as though he could have once been a jockey, so no one doubted his story. His face was thin and gaunt, his complexion sallow, his eyes dark and greedy. His dyed black hair badly needed cutting and treating with a medicated shampoo. The shoulders and lapels of his black porter's jacket were speckled with a heavy dusting of dandruff.

Yes, he knew that Miss Playford's room was on the second floor (he had taken up some extra bath towels, at her request, soon after he had come on duty on Friday night); but there was definitely no sign of Sexton on that floor when he went up with the Belsons' snack at eleven-thirty or thereabouts. In fact he saw no one at all, other than Captain Belson, that is, who answered the door and took in the tray of sandwiches. He was on the second floor for no more than three or four minutes, anyway; the lift remained where he had left it, and he was able to take it straight back down again to the ground floor. He was most emphatic that he did not hear any raised voices while he was up there.

"Silent as the tomb," he assured Walsh. "You could've heard a pin drop!"

"And that," Walsh remarked to Sayer after Ted Black had gone out and closed the door behind him, "simply doesn't ring true to me. What's your opinion of our friend the night porter?"

"Much the same as yours, I should think," Sayer replied with a wry smile. "That stoop of his I'd put down to an occupational disease; he's caught it from spending too much time bending over listening at keyholes."

"Maybe," said Walsh. He folded his arms on the desk and leaned on them. Then, frowning: "If Sexton is our man, then I've a feeling there's a whole lot more to it than a frustrated love affair. Doesn't it strike you as being a pretty drastic thing to do to a lady—chucking her to her death from a cabin lift just because she's given you the brush-off?"

Sayer said noncommittally, "I once heard of a case where a man killed his neighbour in a row over the ownership of a length of rotting hosepipe nobody in his right mind would've wanted."

The telephone rang and Walsh picked up the receiver: Rhys-Williams with his report on his interview with Henry Beamish. The sergeant also relayed some information on Frank Sexton which Walsh had requested.

Replacing the receiver, Walsh said briefly, "Rhys-Williams."

"He's talked to Beamish?"

Walsh nodded. "Beamish could be said to be a little short on alibi. Claims he was working in his garden all day. His wife's bedridden, not got long to go apparently. Beamish says he had lunch with her between twelve and one, but apart from that he worked alone and had no contact with anyone else all day. He complained to Rhys-Williams of a wrenched shoulder, said he got it working in the garden. That might or might not be significant, although he's hardly likely to draw anyone's attention to it if he really got it through heaving his ex-mistress out of a cabin lift. Nothing's been done about Mrs. Beamish, checking out his alibi with her. Not in the circumstances. Rhys-Williams thought he ought to check back with me first. From the way Beamish spoke about his wife, Rhys-Williams said he got the impression that they are pretty close, and that if Beamish is lying about his having had lunch with her, she'll cover for him. Or as the sergeant so charmingly put it, she'll lie like a pig in mud to protect him."

Sayer said thoughtfully, "There's no way really—if Beamish was in Plaid-yro-Wyth yesterday morning and met Cynthia Playford at tenish at the cabin lift—that he could've got back home to London in time for lunch with his wife somewhere around noon. Not even by plane or helicopter. Liverpool would be as near as he could get to Plaid-yro-Wyth by air, and that's over an hour's drive away."

Walsh nodded his endorsement.

"What about the abortion?" asked Sayer. "Did Beamish know about that?"

"Yes. He also admitted that the child was his." Walsh briefly outlined the events preceding the abortion and the reason Beamish had given the sergeant for Cynthia Playford's agreeing to one. "The sterilization op.," he then went on, "came as a bit of a shock, though, Rhys-Williams thought." Walsh leaned back heavily in his chair. "Rhys-Williams didn't think Beamish was all that bothered by his ladylove's untimely passing—found it something of a blessed relief, the sergeant felt." Walsh hesitated. Then: "I had a check run on Sexton . . . There was something familiar about his name; it seemed to ring a bell—" he grinned ruefully at the pun "—somewhere at the back of my mind, but I couldn't quite place it." He rubbed his aching cheekbones wearily; his sinuses were beginning to give him hell. "The name rang a bell all right. From what the sergeant has just told me, I'd say Cynthia Playford was blackmailing Sexton." His head moved slowly from side to side as he said quietly but with feeling, "*Damn!*"

Sayer understood the sentiments behind the Chief Inspector's abrupt outburst. Walsh, he would imagine, felt nothing for the woman Sexton, it now seemed likely, had murdered, nothing for the way he had killed her, nothing for Sexton as a blackmail victim. Blackmailer/blackmail victim—there was little to choose between the two. They usually deserved one another.

Walsh's underlying pity, his regret that soon, probably first thing tomorrow morning, he would almost certainly have to seek a warrant for Sexton's arrest for the murder of Cynthia Playford, related solely to Sexton's wife. The others commit the crimes and her kind paid for them. They would lock Sexton away for a few years, deprive him of his freedom, his fancy silk suits, and the sunlamp Sayer suspected Sexton used to promote that altogether too youthful tan; but it would be Sexton's wife who would pay the real price in terms of misery and suffering and humiliation. She was as much Sexton's victim as Cynthia Playford had been. More so. And where was the justice in that, in arresting Sexton and punishing Mrs. Sexton? This was what Walsh would be asking himself.

There was a knock at the door, to which Walsh responded with a curt, "Come in!"

He didn't recognise the striking, middle-aged woman who entered the room a second later; but it was immediately apparent to him that Sayer knew her and knew her well. She acknowledged the Chief Inspector with a smile; then, looking at Sayer, who had risen and turned to greet her: "I'm very sorry to interrupt you, Superintendent, but I wonder if I might have a word with you. It's rather important."

"If it's about Cynthia Playford, Madame—?" Sayer began, anxious not to usurp Walsh's authority.

She gave Sayer a long, searching look. Then, abruptly, frowning: "No, it's Mrs. Sexton I wished to discuss with you. She's in trouble, Superintendent. Serious trouble. I wanted to ask you if it would be at all possible—" she glanced at Walsh, who was watching and listening to their conversation with a mystified expression on his face "—for the police to provide her with some kind of protection. At least until Cynthia Playford's murderer has been apprehended."

Madame? Walsh's face cleared. The lecturer . . . clairvoyante. Whatever. Walsh, rising and indicating that he wished her to occupy the chair Sayer had left vacant, said, "Madame Herrmann?"

"Mrs. Edwina Charles," Sayer replied for her. "A very good friend of mine."

Walsh gave him a hard look. Good God, the man hadn't gone soft in the head had he, and started consulting fortune tellers?

Sayer completed the introductions. "Chief Inspector Walsh, Madame."

The clairvoyante and the police officer shook hands solemnly, and then they both sat down.

"I've been meaning to have a word with you, Madame . . . er, Mrs. Charles," Walsh said, glancing quickly at Sayer as if hoping for some directive as to how he should address the clairvoyante.

He was indeed in some doubt over the matter and decided to take his cue from Sayer. If Sayer used *madame* again, then so would he.

"Yes," she said quietly, "I thought you might."

CHAPTER 17

There was something unexpected in her voice, just the faintest hint of complicity. The Chief Inspector casually flicked his eyes over Sayer. The same thing was written all over his face. Walsh doubted that Sayer would be party to anything unlawful, but he'd definitely been holding out on him about something. And that something was obviously this woman, her association with Cynthia Playford.

Walsh had noted that once a month in the three months preceding Easter, the clairvoyante's professional name appeared regularly in Cynthia Playford's appointment diary late on a Friday afternoon. There was no way he had been able to tell whether the notation of the clairvoyante's name indicated a visit or a telephone call; and having already been told, more or less in passing, by the president of the Mystic Circle that it was Cynthia Playford who had arranged for Madame Herrmann to lecture at the convention, Walsh would have dismissed the diary notations of her name as being of no other particular significance. However, on moving forward one week to the Friday following Easter, exactly one month since the clairvoyante's name last appeared, it was there again. And that indicated one of two things to Walsh. Either Cynthia Playford and the clairvoyante were good friends, or Cynthia Playford was one of her clients.

He put the question to the clairvoyante, and she confirmed what he had already guessed.

"Why was Miss Playford consulting you?" he then went on to inquire.

Sayer, knowing how stubborn the clairvoyante could be about

some things—her relationship with her clients in particular—dispensed momentarily with the formalities and stepped in quickly. "The Chief Inspector knows about Henry Beamish."

Mrs. Charles nodded. Then she said to Walsh, "In that case, there is little further that I can add, other than to say how extremely distressed Cynthia was about her relationship with this particular man—the hopelessness of the situation in the light of Mrs. Beamish's ill health and her husband's refusal to divorce her on that account."

The clairvoyante read Walsh's next question in his eyes and answered it before he could put it to her. "Although I confirmed that this situation would not alter for some while yet to come, Cynthia continued to consult me in the hope that one day soon I would say yes, all her dreams were now about to come true." She paused and considered the expression of distaste on the Chief Inspector's face—one she was not unfamiliar with. She had yet to meet the police officer who had much of an opinion of clairvoyants and cared for the way they made a living. Including David Sayer. But at least in his case, even if he wasn't always in full agreement with her, he had the common courtesy to listen to what she had to say. This man wouldn't.

Her face hardened a little. "I am no longer concerned about Cynthia Playford, Chief Inspector. She is dead, beyond anyone's help. It is Mrs. Sexton who now needs help. She consulted me privately earlier this afternoon—" The clairvoyante broke off. She could see it was useless; she was simply wasting her breath. . . .

She rose. "Forgive me for boring you, Chief Inspector," she said coolly. "I won't waste any more of your time." Looking directly at Sayer, she then said, quietly and calmly, "There will be another death—one equally as violent as Cynthia Playford's, if not more so. Mrs. Sexton should be kept under close surveillance. She is at very great risk."

The clairvoyante looked back at Walsh. "Good afternoon, Chief Inspector," she said, and turned and walked out.

Walsh returned Sayer's steady gaze unflinchingly. "Well, go

on, say what you've got to say," said the Chief Inspector irritably.

"You've made a big mistake there, Griffith," said Sayer. "You should've listened to her, at least heard her out. Lord knows I don't understand the woman, or what makes her kind tick; but I like and respect her, and you can take my word for it, she's no fool."

Walsh gave him a hard look. "You're not going to tell me you go for all that fortune-telling claptrap?"

"If Edwina Charles says there's going to be another violent death," said Sayer, "then, my friend, you'd better believe it."

Walsh stared at him in disbelief. He was right. Sayer had gone soft in the head. "What d'you expect me to do? Put a twenty-four-hour guard on Mrs. Sexton?" he asked sarcastically.

"You'll regret it if you don't."

Walsh shook his head slowly. "I don't believe any of this."

"No," said Sayer. "That's the pity of it."

Ted Black went about his duties, but kept an eye on the door of the Marlborough Room. The moment he saw the clairvoyante go in, he slipped quickly along to the Wellington Room and glanced in at the bar. Sexton was there. With the president and two or three other conventioneers. Then, turning away, the porter went through the glass swing doors at the far end of the corridor and hurried up the back stairs to the third floor.

Kath Sexton was brushing her hair as the knock came. She turned her head lazily towards the door, gazed at it indifferently for a moment, then looked back at herself in the dressing-table mirror and went on brushing her hair.

Her dark eyes had lost their lustre and become two big black bottomless holes gouged out of her cheekbones. Her hair, with all the brushing it had been given over the past three days, was lank and greasy.

There was another knock, a little more sharp and insistent than before and followed by a man's voice—one she didn't recognise—calling to her by name. She listened for a few moments, then laid down the hairbrush, got up, and crossed unhurriedly to the door.

The night porter had given up and was on his way back to the stairs. He gave a start when he heard her voice. It had a strange quality to it, one that he couldn't define, and it sent chills tingling up his spine.

"Yes?" she said coldly. "You wanted something?"

He turned, smiling uncertainly, and walked slowly back to her. "In a manner of speaking; yes, lady, you might say that."

A note of impatience crept into her voice. "Well, what is it?"

"It's about your husband, lady."

She frowned at him. "My husband? What do you mean?" Her heart gave a sickening thud. *Oh, God, no. They'd arrested him . . . Frank. That was what he'd come to tell her.* She swallowed quickly and laid a hand across her breast as if to still her pounding heart. Her voice was shaky. "Has . . . has something happened to him?"

Ted Black shook his head, smiled again. "No, lady. That's why I'm here, isn't it? To make sure nothing happens to him."

"I don't think I understand you," she said slowly.

"Oh, I think you do, lady." His smile wavered, became sly. "The visit your husband made to Miss Playford's room on Friday night at five and twenty past eleven?" The malicious smirk in his eyes underlined the question in his voice.

She stared at him for a very long moment. Then, stepping back from the door, she said quietly, "You'd better come in."

She went back to the dressing table and sat next to it.

Ted Black closed the door, glancing at her over his shoulder. Then he turned and took a few hesitant steps into the room. He watched her closely. She was making up her mind: deciding what to do, how best to handle the situation. He wasn't too sure himself how to proceed or what would be the better tactic (threats or a more subtle, persuasive approach?); so he decided to wait and let her take the initiative.

"My husband and Miss Playford were very old friends," she

said at length, her tone flat and disinterested. She picked up the hairbrush and began to use it. "There's absolutely no reason at all why he shouldn't have visited her in her room if he so desired."

She stared at the porter in the mirror. "Well?" she demanded.

He grinned. "I'm not arguing with you, lady. You say they were old friends. I believe you."

She stopped brushing her hair and gave him a studied look. "You'll forgive me for being so naive," she said. She paused, then raised the brush and swept back her hair from her face in a defiant gesture. "Is it money you want?"

"Of course," he said, relieved that at last they were getting somewhere. "What else?"

"How much?"

"Let's just say that for the moment that side of it is open to negotiation. Never let it be said that Ted Black is a greedy man."

It was this, of course, the very thing he was so quick to deny about himself, his greed, which really deterred Ted Black from mentioning a definite price outright at this very early stage in the negotiations. That he might set his sights too low didn't bear thinking about. He dropped his head to one side and coolly appraised his victim's worth. He knew money when he saw it, and quality; and this little lady had plenty of both. He grinned crookedly at her. "I'll leave you to discuss the amount with your husband; then when you've fixed on a figure, we'll talk again. I'm quite sure that between the three of us we can come to some sensible arrangement."

Her eyes narrowed. "Why come to me?" she asked curiously. "Why not go direct to my husband with your—" She hesitated; then, as if it were some dirty four-letter word alien to her normal vocabulary and totally repugnant to her: "—*blackmail* threats?"

"Because, lady, you care; and I'm not one hundred per cent sure that the same can be said for your husband. But if you're willing to take that chance, if you think he'll listen to me and see reason and not want to go rushing off and confessing all to the police—"

"No," she said sharply and frowned. "No, don't do that. Leave it to me. I'll talk to him." She moistened her lips. "How do I know that you're not bluffing . . . that what you're saying is the truth?"

"You mean about Miss Playford's threat to expose your husband's involvement in a certain building-society fraud?" The porter's unhesitating reply carried more conviction than it merited. He knew nowhere near as much about Cynthia Playford's blackmail threat as he would have liked to know (what, for example, had been her asking price for *her* silence?) and was largely having to make do as best he could with the meagre scraps of conversation that he had managed to pick up in the few short minutes he had risked being caught lingering in the corridor listening at her door.

Kath's eyes burned into his. "No," she said. Then, hesitantly: "Cynthia wouldn't—"

"Ah, but Cynthia would." The smile on the porter's lips never reached his eyes, which remained alert and watchful. "And Cynthia was going to. Your husband had until the following morning to come across with the goods; and if he didn't, she was going to blow the whistle on him."

"Cynthia wanted money? *From my husband?*" Kath looked and sounded incredulous. "I don't believe it!"

"I never said nothing about her wanting money from him, did I?" This time there was an unmistakably marked hesitancy in the porter's response, but it passed unchallenged. For which he was truly thankful. Her guess was as good as his as to what Cynthia Playford had wanted from her blackmail victim; but somehow Ted Black didn't think it was money.

She stared at him. "She wanted him to—" she hesitated, frowned "—to *marry* her? Divorce me and marry her—is that it?" Kath's voice was bewildered. So were her eyes. "You're telling me that my husband murdered Cynthia Playford because she was threatening to blackmail him if he didn't agree to marry her?"

"No, lady." The porter shook his head slowly. "Your husband

killed Miss Playford because he was an embezzler and she knew it. Pillow talk—isn't that what it's called? The silly little confessions lovers make to one another in the wee small hours of the morning when passion does funny things to a person's better judgment."

There was a long silence. Then Kath nodded. "I see," she said.

"Yes, I'm sure you do." He started to move towards the door. "I'll be in touch."

"No," she said quickly. "I'll contact you. I—it's not going to be easy. I'm going to have to pick my moment. My husband—" She frowned and bit her bottom lip. "He's going through a difficult time right now. You must be reasonable about this."

He paused and turned back to her. "I go off at five A.M. That's as reasonable as I'm prepared to be."

Kath rose protestingly. "It's not enough time." She approached him anxiously. "Please . . . you don't understand. Frank can be difficult, stubborn."

"Five A.M.," he repeated and turned away.

"Please. . . . No, *wait!*" said Kath urgently, shooting out a hand to detain him. He glimpsed the movement out of the corner of his eye; and thinking she was going to strike him, he darted nervily to his right, got his very small feet tangled up first in a piece of loose carpeting and then in one another, and finally crashed bodily against the bathroom door.

The door, which wasn't fully closed, fell open; and losing his balance completely, the porter toppled sideways with it, striking the right side of his neck and head against the edge of the bath. He didn't get up from the floor.

Transfixed, Kath stood perfectly still and stared at him, waiting for him to move or say something. He lay with one shoulder crushed against the bath surround, his head lolling sideways, his eyes half open, his bottom jaw sagging. His short legs, which were crossed and stretched from the bath across the black and white–check vinyl-tiled floor, only barely reached the door. His left trouser leg was slightly wrinkled, revealing that he was wearing short iridescent purple socks with an iridescent green diamond pattern running down the sides of them. They looked awful, bizarre! So did his leg, the inch or so of smooth hairless flesh which she could see between the top of his sock and his trouser cuff. White. Like a small boy's. As if that portion of his flesh had never been exposed to sunlight. For the moment that was all she could think.

She lost track of time. It might have been a mere two minutes later or ten or more, but at length she stepped gingerly over his legs into the bathroom and stood looking down at the side of his face.

Her pulse rate quickened and she felt herself slowly coming back to life. He was dead. His neck, she guessed. He must have broken it when his head struck the edge of the bath.

Her breathing was quick now and shallow. The room began to pulsate round her. She closed her eyes, put her hands to her temples, and pressed hard with her fingertips. She had to calm down . . . *think!* This could be the best thing that could've happened. But she had to keep calm and work things out carefully in her head.

Abruptly she dropped her hands, turned, then stepped back over the porter's legs and went to the door and depressed the tiny button in the centre of the aluminium knob, double-locking it. She had scarcely finished doing this when she heard someone —her husband, she thought—turning a key in the lock.

Sexton persisted with his key for a moment or two, then guessed what was wrong and called to his wife to let him in.

She flattened back against the wall of the bathroom, holding her breath. The doorknob moved from side to side as her husband tried it.

"Kath," he called to her again. "Are you in there? It's me, Frank. Let me in, will you? You've locked the door; I can't get in."

She swallowed loudly, her eyes fixed mesmerically on the smeary knob. A minute passed; then she heard her husband walk away and, a moment later, the sound of the lift starting up.

She waited for several moments; then, without looking at what lay on the bathroom floor, she made her way unsteadily into the main room and sat on the foot of one of the beds. Automatically, she reached over to the dressing table, picked up the hairbrush, and started using it. She gazed steadfastly at the telephone, almost as if she expected it to ring at any moment; and sure enough, half a dozen brushstrokes later, it pealed shrilly. Once. Then, after a short delay, a second time.

She ignored it, went on brushing her hair. It would be Frank, getting someone at the desk to check if she were there. It didn't really matter who it was. She wasn't going to talk to anyone, least of all to him, until she had had time to think things out.

She had more or less decided what she was going to do. She was physically strong for a woman. Before her marriage she had been a psychiatric nurse and was therefore properly trained in manhandling deadweights from one place to another—full-grown adults at that, not men in little boys' bodies, and the porter wasn't much more than a boy in build. She knew that she could move him from the bathroom. But where to? The back stairs? She measured the distance from the room to the rear staircase in her mind's eye. If she could get him there, then tumble him down the steps, the police would think that was how he got the broken neck. *Shoelaces.* . . . Was he wearing that kind of shoe or a slip-on? She couldn't remember offhand; she'd have to check. . . .

She frowned thoughtfully. No, the rear staircase was out. It was too far away. She'd make it all right with him, even if she couldn't lift him and had to drag him all the way; but she'd be seen. People, like Frank, would be coming up to their rooms now to change for the banquet. *The lift?* She could wait until someone brought it up; then when they had gone into their room, she could—

No, that wouldn't work, either. Halfway there, in the middle of no-man's-land, the lift might suddenly take off. Someone would have to hold it for her. *Nigel?*

She looked at the telephone and frowned again. Wouldn't the simplest thing be to tell the police the truth—ring down and say there had been an accident? (Which there had; she'd never laid a finger on the man!)

No, it wouldn't be left simply at that. The police would want to know what he was doing in the room in the first place. She'd seen the look on that policeman's face when he'd been showing Captain and Mrs. Belson out. He knew Frank had killed Cynthia. (*God, everyone knew it, even Mrs. Belson!*) This would be handing him Frank's head on a plate.

She heard a faint sound and gave a start, looking round nervously over her shoulder at the bathroom. Then, dropping the hairbrush onto the floor, she let out a sharp gasp. Standing groggily in the bathroom doorway, ruefully rubbing the side of his neck, was the porter—very much alive, if not quite intact. He staggered a few steps forward. Kath screamed.

"Christ, lady!" he muttered. "Turn it down, will you? D'you want to bring the whole bleedin' police force up here?"

Her hand over her mouth, eyes glazed with shock, she watched him lower himself onto the edge of the other bed.

"I—I thought . . ." she stammered, "I thought you were—" She didn't finish.

"Chance'd be a fine thing," he said, grinning a little. "For you, that is, lady. Take more'n a little tap on the side of the head to finish me off. Ten-ton truck more like!"

Suddenly he was back on his feet again. Then, drunkenly, still rubbing his neck, he stumbled across the room, letting himself out without another word.

Kath sat for a long time staring at the closed door; then, with a shaking hand, she bent down and picked up the brush and reapplied it to her hair.

CHAPTER 18

Sayer found Mrs. Charles in the small lounge off reception. He had abandoned all hope of talking Walsh round. But he had tried; spent over half an hour arguing with Walsh; tried to convince him that he should talk again with the clairvoyante who had worked in the past in close association, Sayer assured Walsh, with other senior police officers on murder investigations where, he insisted, her counsel, albeit unorthodox, had proved most successful. To no avail.

"I'm sorry about that," he said apologetically, positioning a comfortable leather armchair so that he and the clairvoyante could sit facing one another. "Walsh is a damned fool."

"He thinks he knows who killed Cynthia Playford, doesn't he?" she said.

Sayer gave her a sharp look and she smiled faintly. "He would've been far more receptive had he not believed he knew who murdered her." The clairvoyante's dark blue eyes clouded. "But for some curious reason—a reason I can't even understand or explain to myself—it isn't going to make a jot of difference."

"You mean Walsh's knowing who killed Cynthia Playford isn't going to prevent another murder taking place?"

The clairvoyante avoided a direct answer. "As you and the Chief Inspector have obviously discussed the case at depth, and as I'm sure he's confided in you as to the identity of the person whom he believes to be Cynthia Playford's killer, I'll tell you what I saw in the immediate future for Mrs. Sexton. Then if, as I've surmised, you know whom the Chief Inspector suspects, you should be able to answer that question for yourself."

He nodded his agreement.

"I saw a man, Superintendent—a man in danger, terribly afraid of something."

His quick nod implied that this made sense; it fitted in with what he knew of the matter.

She went on, "The man was running. . . ."

Again Sayer nodded. Though it was a moot point whether Sexton would be the kind who would run or not; but he'd certainly be afraid.

"Running," the clairvoyante continued, "from Mrs. Sexton."

Sayer gave her a puzzled look. Why would Sexton be running away from his wife . . . afraid? Because he'd killed her? Was this why Mrs. Charles had wanted police protection for Mrs. Sexton?

"But why would Sexton want to kill his wife?" Without realising it, Sayer asked the question of himself out loud.

The clairvoyante's eyebrows rose. "Sexton?"

Sayer looked quickly round, but there was no one else within earshot. Most of the conventioneers were in their rooms, changing for the banquet.

"It looks that way," he went on in a quick undertone. "Walsh is pretty sure Cynthia Playford was blackmailing him."

Mrs. Charles did not seem surprised.

"You think it was a possibility too?" he inquired.

"When a person is as emotionally unstable as Cynthia was, anything is possible, Superintendent," replied the clairvoyante. "But it is certainly something of which I have no definite knowledge—if that's what you're wondering. I only learnt of their— Cynthia and Frank Sexton's—involvement with one another yesterday. Cynthia never once mentioned his name to me."

Sayer was thoughtful. He spoke slowly. "I could understand Sexton killing his wife at the height of his affair with Cynthia Playford, but why now? It doesn't make sense."

"Maybe the man I saw in the crystal wasn't Frank Sexton."

"You didn't see him clearly?"

"Not his physical features. It was just a fleeting, though nonetheless vivid picture, the spectre of a male figure in some considerable fear fleeing from Mrs. Sexton."

"And you think this man—whoever he is—poses some threat to her?"

The clairvoyante did not answer immediately. Then, in a slow, thoughtful voice: "Or she, in some way, to him."

"Could you tell where this . . . this whatever it is you're afraid is going to happen involving Mrs. Sexton will take place?"

The clairvoyante looked at him for a moment, then gazed past him into the distance. Slowly it came back to her: the man, his fear. . . .

"I see a wide open space," she said. "Dark and yet not dark."

"A wide open space," he repeated musingly. "Out-of-doors?"

The clairvoyante continued to gaze unblinkingly into the distance. "Yes and no," she replied at length. "It will not happen as it happened before with Cynthia Playford, out there in the mountains, the valleys. I see level ground, a great expanse of it. . . ."

Several women came laughing into the lounge and the clairvoyante gave a start; looked quickly at Sayer. "I'm sorry; there's nothing more I can tell you."

He frowned. "You're sure it isn't going to happen here—" he waved an arm in the air "—in the hotel?" He lowered his voice considerably. "What I mean is, Sexton isn't going to harm her when they're alone together in their room?"

Mrs. Charles shook her head. "No, Superintendent, that was not my impression at all."

"Then Mrs. Sexton is safe for tonight. What with the banquet and the floor show afterwards—"

The lounge was becoming crowded with conventioneers seeking a prebanquet drink.

"I've got myself a bolt-hole in a small hotel down the road; we'll meet here after breakfast in the morning," Sayer suggested. "And in the meanwhile I'll try and get hold of a local map, and we'll see if you can pinpoint this wide open space you say you saw."

They rose and went into reception where Sayer paused and said, "Until morning, then. . . ."

She nodded, watched him cross reception to the revolving door to the street where, instead of continuing, he hesitated and looked back. The clairvoyante was still watching him. There was an odd expression on her face, no response to the quick parting smile he gave her. He continued to watch her, a sinking feeling in the pit of his stomach. She hadn't told him everything; there was something else, something she was deliberately keeping from him. His thoughts immediately went back several years to another conversation they had once had about a spectre she had seen in the crystal. In that instance, the spectre had concerned herself—in fact it had been a spectre of herself wearing a valuable piece of jewellery belonging to a murder victim which had later proved to be the key to the crime.

Sayer, a worried expression on his face, stepped out into the still, cold night air. Frank Sexton had no more murdered Cynthia Playford than he had, and the clairvoyante knew it.

Mrs. Charles did not attend the banquet. She remained all evening in her room, sitting motionless in the dark in an easy chair with her eyes closed and her mind focused steadily on the spectre of her dead mother's face. As the hours passed and her conscious mind became more and more exhausted, her subconscious came gradually to the fore and with it, at 3 A.M., the answer she sought.

Leaning sideways, she switched on a table lamp, then rose and went to her suitcase, and removed a bulky envelope from one of the satiny blue pockets in its lining. She gazed at the envelope in her hand for some considerable time before opening it. This was the connection—not between her mother and Kath Sexton, as she had at first mistakenly thought, but between herself, her mother, and Cynthia Playford.

A little over an hour later, at four-thirty, Kath Sexton quietly left her bed and groped her way soundlessly to the chair by the window where she had left her clothes neatly laid out ready for this moment.

She pulled on a dark pair of slacks over her pyjamas and without removing her pyjama top, slipped her head and arms into a black polo-neck sweater. Her shoes were waiting, tucked tidily under the chair, and she slid her bare feet quickly into them.

Turning, she stood for a moment listening to her husband's breathing. It was even, heavier than usual. He was not a light sleeper, but to make sure of it she had slipped two of her sleeping pills into his coffee after the banquet.

She moved to the curtains and parted them so that she could see the time by her wristwatch. She had twenty-five minutes, plenty of time, to go down the back stairs and out to the expansive, ramshackle galvanized-iron shed at the rear of the hotel which the management euphemistically referred to as "the garage."

The small side door off reception would have been left open; the night porter had agreed to take care of that for her. She was to slip out to the garage and wait for him there. His car was the grey Ford Escort which she would find parked on its own in the far right-hand corner. It would be left unlocked so that if she were to get there first she could climb inside out of the cold.

She checked the time again. Four-forty. Time she was making a move.

She returned to her bed and swiftly rearranged the pillows and bedding to look as though someone were lying there sleeping (just in case Frank should wake up and notice that her bed was empty and wonder where she was); then she crossed silently to her husband's bedside table, carefully extricated his car keys and the key to the room from his loose change, and then quietly went out, closing the door gently behind her.

She neither saw anybody nor heard anything more alarming than muted distant coughing, and some twelve or so minutes later, her teeth chattering with nervous excitement, she stepped into the yawning shadowy chasm beyond the gloomily lit yard to the rear of the hotel and looked around for her husband's Datsun. He had used it since they had arrived, so it wasn't where he had parked it originally but to one side near the back.

Going over to it, she unlocked it and got inside, shivering as the damp cold of the vinyl seat penetrated the thin fabric of her slacks and the back of her sweater. The engine started on her second attempt, idled for a moment, then faded away. She tried again, quickly adjusted the choke, relaxed as the engine picked up momentum; then, reversing out of the parking space, she swung the wheel hard to the right and backed up against the rear wall. The front of the car was now facing the hangarlike entrance to the garage—there was no front wall as such, no doorway, just a wide open space giving out on to the yard.

She let the engine idle, so quietly that one would have had to listen carefully or place a hand on the gently vibrating bonnet to know that the motor was running; and soon the car was warm. But her teeth still chattered. With nothing further to do for the moment, her thoughts began to drift. . . .

Ted, was that his name? Yes, that was what he'd called himself. Ted, then. . . . The moment he crossed the yard she would see him silhouetted in the entrance against the thin yellow glow from the solitary light that was left on all night at the back of the hotel. She let her right foot brush the accelerator pedal, and the engine responded with a gentle purr. She wouldn't be able to see his face, not with his back to the light. She hoped not, anyway. She thought about the look in his eye when she had spoken to him at the desk shortly before eleven that night and arranged with him to meet when he came off duty at five in the morning. There had been something about his expression, a kind of little-boy-greedy anticipation which had reminded her of the look in Frank's eye when he had been going out to meet Cynthia Playford. She had always known when he was going to meet her. Just by looking in his eyes. There were other things she could tell about Frank too, just by looking in his eyes. Such as when the fight was going out of him or when he was going to give up. He'd given up over Lucy. Refused to do anything about the maniac who ran her down, never even so much as claimed compensation for her smashed bicycle.

Tears stung the back of Kath's eyes and she gripped the steering wheel tightly. Well, this time it was going to be different. Frank could get that look out of his eye—he wasn't going to give up; she wasn't going to let him take the easy way out. Not this time. She had let him have his way over Lucy's accident; listened to him and tried to understand what he'd meant when he'd said that an eye for an eye was just that, no more, no less, that no one really won; put the feelings of the family of their baby's killer first when all she really cared about and wanted was just retribution for herself and Frank for the beautiful young life that had been snatched from them forever.

She rubbed the sleeve of her sweater quickly across her damp eyes and set her jaw squarely. She was never going to suffer again, was never again going to let anybody take away from her someone she loved. Frank had no right to expect it of her. He owed it to her for all the hurt and humiliation not to confess to Cynthia Playford's murder. She would throw his argument over Lucy back in his face. What was done was done. Over. Finished. Best forgotten. No one could say Cynthia hadn't deserved to die. She was a husband stealer; a common, incestuous whore; a dirty blackmailer. And there was only one way to pay off a blackmailer. . . .

The outline of a man walking with a quick urgency suddenly flitted across the pale yellow back cloth and Kath stiffened. She depressed the clutch pedal and put the car in gear. Her hands were sweaty, and she momentarily released her grip on the steering wheel to let the air get at them. Her heart thudded dully in her breast. It was now or never. He was getting too close. A few more yards and he would see her—

As if abruptly transported beyond that time and place and no longer in any way involved with or responsible for anything that might be about to happen, she listened to the roar of the engine and the protesting squeal of rubber as the Datsun lunged forward. Her right foot was almost to the floor; her arms cramped agonisingly under the strain of her relentless vicelike grip on the wheel. Her eyes watered and ached painfully. And then the inevitable impact, the short, narrow, planklike shape flying through the air and striking the windscreen, remaining there hard against it for a moment in suspended animation, then flopping backwards, slithering across the bonnet, and disappearing from view down the near side of the car.

She hit the brakes hard and sat there, still gripping the wheel, shaking uncontrollably, the neck of her sweater clinging uncomfortably to her sticky, prickling throat, perspiration trickling from her armpits.

Would it happen again? The same thing that had happened before in the bathroom? A few minutes' unconsciousness and then he'd get staggering to his feet, the indestructible man?

She held her breath and waited, a scream waiting at the back of her throat, should he suddenly loom at the side window.

Nothing happened. Five, maybe ten minutes later (time meant nothing to her anymore), very carefully, she backed the car up and then switched on the headlights.

It could almost have been the final closing scene of a stage tragedy—the principal actor lying on his side in the harsh, glaring white spotlight, one leg crossed over the other, his right arm flung abandonedly above his head as if it might have been broken in more than one place; his eyes wide open, startled, disbelieving, staring straight at his killer. His mouth too was wide open and shaped around a mute scream of sudden shock. It both repelled and fascinated the woman in the car. Had he realised, too late, that he himself, with his feeble joke about a ten-ton truck, had suggested the best way to be rid of him? Had he suddenly seen what she had realised while he had lain unconscious on the bathroom floor—that death was and should be the only sensible and reasonable payoff he would ever get from the Sextons?

Kath switched off the headlights, put the car in gear, turned the steering wheel slightly to the left, moved slowly forward, then put her foot down hard, bouncing in her seat and rocking forward until her forehead almost struck the steering wheel as first the front wheels then the rear ones passed over the night porter's body, crushing his chest and legs. She drove on for a short distance, then stopped the car. Opening the glove compartment, she felt around quickly, found what she wanted, a flashlight; then she got out.

Her knees unexpectedly gave way as she went to stand up and she collapsed on all fours. The flashlight rolled out of reach under a parked car, and for the moment she could do nothing but remain where she was on her hands and knees, trembling violently. She waited for a few minutes, until the trembling stopped; then still on all fours, she crawled forward like a baby towards the other car and retrieved the flashlight, made sure that it wasn't broken.

Reaching cautiously up the side of the car and gripping the door handle, she hauled herself onto her feet, falling back against it with an exhausted gasp which sent a searing pain through her chest. She clutched at the front of her sweater, for a moment too scared to breathe normally lest the pain should return. Then, becoming anxious about time (it seemed like hours, not minutes, since she had left the hotel room), she forced herself to put a tentative foot forward, then another one and another one, until finally she was standing over the porter's badly crushed body.

He had been dragged over onto his back and was lying now with his legs going out at odd angles to his body as if they too might be broken in more than one place. He looked like some grotesque marionette, double-jointed at the elbows, hips, and knees; carelessly tossed to one side between performances.

She flashed a beam of light onto his face. Blood had trickled from his mouth and run down his chin and neck to the back of his collar and formed a small pool in a crumbling hollow in the badly disintegrating concrete floor beneath his head. She breathed in deeply and a shiver went through her. He wouldn't be getting up and going anywhere ever again. He was dead. This time she was sure of it.

Tucking the flashlight into the elasticized waistband of her slacks, she then reached under his armpits and dragged him slowly over to the Datsun, shuffling round with him until he was parallel with the boot of the car. Then she let him fall back onto the floor and got the keys to unlock the boot.

The boot open, she got behind him again and with her hands once more securely gripping him under his armpits, she raised his shoulders, then the upper half of his trunk until, with a slight twist, he pitched forward headfirst into the boot. The weightier, upper half of his body was now lying face down in the boot, his abdomen resting across the back of the car, his legs outside it, and his feet brushing the floor.

She took a rest, leaning for several moments against the back of the car panting heavily, her lungs feeling as if they would burst. She was nowhere near as fit as she had imagined; her nursing years were a long way in the past. Then, taking several deep breaths, she summoned up all her strength, bent over and wrapped her arms around his small legs, and on the second attempt, successfully hoisted the rest of him into the boot.

Doubled over him, panting breathlessly, she grabbed hold of the raised lid above her head and waited for her strength to return. She felt wobbly all over, didn't dare to move. Eventually her breathing became quieter, her body less like a stranger's and more her own again. She straightened up cautiously, waited for any adverse reaction. She moistened her lips—she had been breathing mostly through her mouth, which had dried them out. Yes, she was fine now. No giddiness, just a little weakness still in the knees, some soreness in her arms and shoulders. Must hurry now. . . .

With slightly shaking hands, she covered the porter with an old brown travelling rug, made some hasty adjustments to one of his legs, the foot of which was sticking out at an awkward angle; then she reached behind the spare wheel for the plastic water container and the bundle of old rags which her husband always carried about with him for an emergency. There was even a spade tucked down the other side, part of his snow-survival kit. Luckily he hadn't got round to taking it out.

It was getting light but she used the flashlight to pick out her way back across the floor to where the porter had lain; then, placing the flashlight on the floor and working by its light, she poured a good measure of water from the container into the pool of blood where his head had rested, diluting it. Using some of the rag as a floor cloth and taking care not to splash herself, she dipped the rag into the watery pool of blood and spread it out evenly beyond the hollow in a wide, sweeping semicircle, finally drying off the floor vigorously with the remainder of the rag.

Picking up the flashlight, she then checked carefully all round the floor to see if she had missed any blood spots. There were several at the back of the Datsun, and she quickly sponged them up with the wet rag and then dried them off. When she had done this, she tucked the water container and the soiled bundle of rags under the rug with the dead man, then closed the lid of the boot.

She leant on it for a few moments, her eyes closed tightly against the sudden sting of perspiration; then she walked unsteadily round to the front of the car and ran the flashlight over it. There was a small dent in the bumper bar slightly off-centre, but no other damage that she could discern. The dent might have already been there; she wasn't sure. Then she checked the bonnet and the windscreen, and finally the nearside. All okay. But first thing after breakfast tomorrow (today, that is), she would take the car down to that coin-operated car wash she had noticed on their way in and give it a good clean. Just in case she had missed something.

She snapped off the flashlight and went round to the other side of the car, climbed in, and then replaced the flashlight in the glove compartment.

She had thought very carefully about this part—what she should do next, how best to get rid of the body. Her original plan had been to drive, there and then, somewhere out into the countryside and dig a shallow grave for it with the spade, then to return the car to the garage and carry on as normal.

But that wouldn't work. Five-thirty A.M. wasn't as early as some people thought. She had had enough sleepless nights in her time to know just how many people there were about at this hour of the morning. It was too risky to do anything with the body straightaway. She would have to leave it. Put the car back where Frank had left it; return to their room. Wait. She would have to tell Frank about it, of course: there was no way around that; and then together, later, they would decide what should be done—whether they would delay leaving Plaid-yro-Wyth for London until nightfall and bury the body in some isolated spot along the way, or get rid of it sometime during the day, before they left.

Everything was going to be all right. Frank would see that it had been the only way, that all he had to do now was to keep quiet.

A surge of elation went through her. Nobody now, nobody save themselves, knew that Frank had gone to Cynthia's room on Friday night. Nobody would ever know. He was safe. And she'd done it; she'd saved him!

Shivering with excitement, she started up the car and reversed back into its previous parking space. Fifteen minutes later, at five forty-five by her watch, she was back in the hotel room, undressing.

Her husband slept on peacefully.

CHAPTER 19

The door of the Marlborough Room was wide open. Nigel Playford could see Walsh sitting at the desk looking at some photo-
graphs in a file. Another plainclothes detective—Sergeant Rhys-
Williams—was leaning over his shoulder pointing something out
to him. Walsh closed the file, and the two police officers looked
up, as if suddenly alerted by some hidden warning device that
someone was spying on them.

"Ah, Mr. Playford," said Walsh musically. He inched the file
aside and the sergeant drifted over to the fireplace where he
stood at ease with his hands clasped loosely behind his back.
"Good morning. Do come in."

Nigel stepped forward hesitantly. "I'm sorry if I've interrupted
something important. I just wondered if you'd—" He left the sentence unfinished.

Walsh waved him over to the empty chair near the desk and
then, when Nigel left the door wide open, motioned to Rhys-
Williams to close it. He leaned back expansively in his chair.
There were dark circles under his eyes, but overall he was looking a little better and felt it.

"No, no news, I'm afraid, Mr. Playford. That was what you
wanted to know, wasn't it? No one specific person is helping us
with our inquiries, as the newspapers say."

"I was wondering—" Nigel paused, frowned. "I should really
be getting back to London today. I've got a column to write."

Walsh nodded his head. "I think that'll be in order. For you to
leave. We've got your address should we need to talk to you
again."

Nigel considered him thoughtfully. There was something

different about him. He looked tired, but there was a purposefulness about his manner that hadn't been evident at yesterday's interview. "You know who killed my sister, don't you?" Nigel held up a hand. "You don't have to say anything; it isn't necessary. I know, you see: I've always known. I don't suppose—" He paused; eyed Walsh speculatively. Then: "No, you can't. I mustn't ask what it was all about." He shook his head slowly. "I've known all along that it was Frank Sexton. It had to be him. That business over the raincoat . . . you know all about that, don't you?" He smiled ruefully. "And his affair with my sister?"

Walsh nodded, and after a moment so did Nigel. "Silly thing to do, I know . . . pretending his coat was mine. Sorry about that—" he shrugged "—but I did it for her, for Mrs. Sexton. I felt I owed her. That was why I couldn't tell you about Cynthia and Frank. It had to come from someone else, not me. But I wouldn't really expect anyone to understand—" His voice tailed off.

Walsh motioned to Nigel, who had remained standing, to be seated. "There was just one thing, Mr. Playford, while you're here. Was your sister in any financial difficulty?"

"Cynthia?" Nigel looked surprised. He sat down, frowning. "Not so far as I know. Why do you ask?"

Ignoring the question, Walsh said, "Would it be the sort of thing your sister would've discussed with you?"

"Yes, I think so. Why not? If she was in some kind of jam, financially, that is—and for the life of me I can't think how she'd get herself into that sort of mess (an emotional tangle, maybe, but not a financial one; Cynthia had a good business head on her shoulders)—she'd have known that she could turn to me for help. Any number of people, friends, would've been willing to give her a loan to tide her over a rough patch. Including Frank Sexton, even though it was all over between them—as far as Cynthia was concerned, anyway. They were still friends. Cynthia's love affairs always ended that way, with the guy still in love with her and taking on the role of Sir Galahad, a knight in shining white armour just hoping and praying the fair damsel would find herself in some distress and turn back to him for help. Insane as it may sound in the circumstances, in their own peculiar way, Cynthia and Frank really were friends, good friends. Cynthia didn't fall out with her ex-lovers. That's the one thing that doesn't make sense about Frank. . . ."

Walsh let Nigel have his head. Nigel was a little more introspective today, a lot less pleased with himself; and now that he had given up trying to be clever, he might even prove to be of some real use to him.

Walsh was convinced that there was blackmail at the bottom of Sexton's late-night visit to Cynthia Playford's hotel room. But after having lain awake for most of the night thinking about it, he wasn't wholly convinced that this was solely why he had killed her. He had conferred at length with the Chief Constable on this point first thing that morning, though he suspected he had failed to convince his superior that there was still something else, something missing, the x-factor that had transformed Sexton from a blackmail victim into a callous murderer.

The blackmail motive was still very much open to speculation, anyway; Walsh had no real proof as yet that Cynthia Playford had unearthed some hard evidence of Sexton's complicity in a building-society fraud as opposed to his merely confessing his guilt to her. And if this were the case, if Cynthia Playford had threatened to expose him on the strength of his verbal confession alone, then he would simply deny everything just as he had when the massive fraud had first been uncovered. So she must have dug up some very definite physical evidence of the part he had played in the fraud.

But why research into his building-society activities in the first place? Professional curiosity? For the sole purpose of blackmailing him at some later date, should she so desire?

Of the two motives, curiosity seemed the more likely. It certainly seemed in keeping with her character. But if her brother were right about her and Sexton's being good friends, despite all outward appearances to the contrary (and Nigel had again returned to this theme, repeating almost word for word what he had said earlier about the nature of his sister's relationship with

Sexton after they broke up), and she had no financial problems, why should the not unnatural curiosity of a professional researcher have suddenly become supplanted by a criminal urge to try one's hand at blackmail? It didn't add up. There was definitely something missing, some factor he hadn't considered. . . .

Walsh permitted Nigel to finish what he was saying; then he asked, "Can you tell me what your sister was working on at the time of her death?"

Nigel made a face and shook his head. "No idea— She didn't discuss her work with me. All those facts and endless details she used to bury herself in bored me to tears."

"She enjoyed her work?"

"Some of it. The things she could really get her teeth into. Mostly it was all pretty deadly dull routine stuff, you know. . . . Researching obscure poets who were long since dead and never wrote anything worthwhile remembering when they were alive, anyway. That sort of thing. But occasionally she'd get a commission that would really excite her interest and she'd go underground. I wouldn't hear anything from her for ages, not until she'd got it all sorted out. Though that didn't happen often."

"Anything recently?"

Nigel gave him a careful look. "Maybe; I'm not sure. She'd been acting so peculiarly lately over Henry Beamish, her doctor boyfriend, that I can't be certain that it wasn't that. Or, now that I know about it, the abortion you said she'd had. That makes some women go a bit funny-peculiar, doesn't it? Not act normally."

"Your sister hadn't, in your opinion, been behaving normally lately?"

"Well, no—not now that I come to think about it. Not for a couple of months. But then that would coincide with the abortion, wouldn't it? And she certainly hadn't been looking too well these past couple of months. I noticed it particularly while we were driving here on Friday."

Walsh nodded. "I wonder if you could think hard, Mr. Playford, and try, if you can, to divorce yourself from the abortion

and be a little more objective about the change you'd observed
in your sister?"

Nigel was quiet for a moment. Then, shaking his head: "It really only walks us round in the same tired old circle with Henry
Beamish standing squarely in the middle of it. I honestly think
she was going to pieces over him; in fact on Friday night it even
crossed my mind that she might be well on her way to a nervous
breakdown over their bust-up. We had quite a row . . . over one
of the contestants in yesterday's competition. Lord knows why,
but Cynthia really had it in for the poor girl. I admit that
Cynthia could be pretty spiteful when the mood took her, but
this was bloody ridiculous, childish; and to my eternal regret, I
was just as childish back. I deliberately said things that weren't
true just to make her angry. Alison Crosby, the magicienne who
won yesterday's contest?" He widened his eyes interrogatively,
and Walsh nodded. "I pretended she was granting me certain
favours in return for services rendered in connection with her career." He paused, frowned. "Stupid of me, I know; I realise that
now. But at the time, she got me so mad at her that I felt it
served her right. She was so Bolshie about it—with everyone."

"With everyone, Mr. Playford?"

"Yes," he sighed. "When she wasn't having a go at me, she
was needling Headley, our president—she'd never forgiven him
for being one of those who pulled her off Kath Sexton when they
had a public brawl one time over Frank; and once Cynthia got
going, she could really cover some territory. Headley has since
said to me that he felt Cynthia came here this weekend spoiling
for a fight; and I think he was right there, though wrong perhaps
in thinking she was specifically looking for trouble with Kath
Sexton." He hesitated and frowned again. "Poor Kath. I was for-
getting her. God knows what this will do to her, how she'll cope
when you arrest Frank. You people are hardened to this sort of
thing; you don't know the hell we ordinary mortals go through at
times like these. This will be the second major blow she's had to
bear. You try imagining what it must be like to lose somebody
you love."

"It's perhaps not so difficult for me as you might think, Mr. Playford," said Walsh.

Nigel laughed dryly. "All right then, you tell me what it's like to lose a child, an only child, in a road accident like Frank and Kath Sexton did."

Rhys-Williams looked quickly at Walsh, to whom a similar tragedy had occurred involving his youngest child less than two years ago; but Walsh merely looked mildly curious and asked, "How long ago?"

"Eight years. Lucy, their daughter, would've been sixteen this year. Kath's never got over it. Not in my opinion. And this, taking Frank from her, will finish her."

Walsh raised his eyebrows. "Let's hope she's tougher than you think, Mr. Playford. Women are generally much more resilient than men suppose."

"You hope!" Nigel retorted sharply. "You don't know how hard I've prayed, for Kath's sake, that it wasn't Frank who killed my sister. Anybody but him. She's suffered enough."

There was a timid knock at the door which the sergeant answered. Mrs. Belson smiled diffidently at him; and then, glancing round him at Walsh and seeing Nigel Playford, she said apologetically, "Oh, I'm terribly sorry; you're busy, Chief Inspector. I'll come back later when you're free."

"I was just leaving," said Nigel, rising. He smiled at Walsh and extended a limp hand, nodded at Mrs. Belson. Then, with a flickering glance Rhys-Williams' way, he went out.

"Please sit down, Mrs. Belson," said Walsh.

"No, I won't if you don't mind," she said quickly. "I've only popped in to ask if it'll be all right for my husband and me to return to London. He's—" She faltered; sighed a little. "He had a very bad night, and I really think we ought to get home as quickly as possible." She smiled wistfully. "He's dying, you know. A month; two at the most."

Walsh frowned. "I'm sorry."

She had remained hesitant about coming right into the room; but now she moved, halving the distance between herself and the Chief Inspector almost as if to avoid being overheard by anyone out in the corridor. She even lowered her voice—in sorrow, as it turned out. "He had an operation two years ago; but it was too late, I'm afraid."

Walsh came slowly round the desk to her. "Is there anything I can do? Will you be all right?"

"Perfectly, thank you," she said composedly. "I do all the driving, anyway. It'll be all right? For us to leave?"

Walsh nodded and said, "Yes, of course, whenever you wish," and went with her to the door. The smile she gave him before turning away was inordinately sad.

"Terrific!" said Rhys-Williams as Walsh turned back. "There goes our only witness. Our whole case."

"Nothing we can do about it, lad," said Walsh complacently. "Death waits in the wings for no man indefinitely and cares not for the police and their problems."

"Worthwhile, d'you think, rummaging around to see if anybody else spotted Sexton going up to Cynthia Playford's room on Friday night?"

"Not even Belson saw him do that," Walsh reminded him. "He could've only ever given the lie to Sexton's claim that he returned immediately to the party after going to the phone to speak to her."

"Looks like our only hope is a confession," said Rhys-Williams.

"We might be lucky. Once Sexton knows, or thinks we know he went up to her room that night, he might break down and come clean."

"Not with his form, he won't. He's going to be a tough nut to crack."

"You really think so?"

"Don't you?"

Walsh thought for a moment. "Up to a point. I think his wife's tougher. You heard what the man said about her, what she's been through—"

"Bloody insensitive swine," muttered Rhys-Williams. "Talking like that to you."

"There was no way Playford could've known about my child," said Walsh. He sighed and nodded his head. "Just thank God for it, lad—that they do talk to us that way. Our job wouldn't be half so easy if it weren't for the insensitive Nigel Playfords of this world who open their great big fat mouths—" he smiled faintly "—and talk and talk and talk until finally—if we get really lucky! —they find something worthwhile to say."

The sergeant gave him a penetrating look. "I hadn't noticed it. . . . That we have it particularly easy."

"We get there, lad; we get there," sighed Walsh. "In the end."

CHAPTER 20

"So this is it, eh?" said Sexton dully. "I expected you would in the finish."

"What's that, Mr. Sexton?" inquired Walsh. This was getting to be a habit. Playford, now Sexton, putting their own interpretation on events, jumping to conclusions, assuming too much. They were so sure they had all the answers. It was a pity he couldn't share their confidence and be as certain as they were that theirs were the right ones.

Sexton frowned; his voice prickled with intense irritation. "I'd rather we didn't play games, if you don't mind. Either you charge me straightaway with having committed some crime, or I walk right out that door—" he jerked his head angrily over his shoulder "—here and now."

Walsh seemed to consider the possibility, as if charging Sexton were something that had not occurred to him but mightn't be a bad idea.

There was a glazed look to Sexton's eyes. He looked as though he hadn't slept properly, if at all. The anger left him as suddenly as it had come. He spoke in a dull monotone again, and gripped the back of the chair which separated him from the desk and Walsh as though he would use it to defend himself should the other man give him the slightest provocation. "This is like a crime novel I remember once reading where the reader was privy to all the chief character's crimes, all of which he got away with until right at the very last moment when he's arrested and convicted for a crime he never committed."

"That's how you see yourself, is it?" asked Walsh.

"If you arrest me for Cynthia Playford's murder, yes. It's

ironic, really," said Sexton with a sardonic smile. "Poetic justice, if you like, that this is how I should finish up . . . charged with murder. Any one of a number of other crimes, but not that, murder. I'd laugh if only it weren't so bloody pathetic."

"That was Miss Playford's hold over you, was it? These other crimes you mentioned?"

Sexton laughed bitterly. "There's no point in the kid-glove treatment now, Chief Inspector; it's a little late in the day for that, isn't it? Cynthia Playford knew I was an embezzler."

Walsh frowned and went to speak, but Sexton wearily waved the interruption aside.

"No, never mind the caution, Chief Inspector. I'll make a full statement; be happy to. Just let me talk; get this out of my system." He drew out the chair and sat down. He spoke dejectedly. "Cynthia knew that I, while chairman of the board of directors of a certain building society, had defrauded that society of a very considerable sum of money over a long period of time, and that by mutual agreement—and in consideration of another large sum of money paid by me—my co-conspirator, the building society's chief accountant, who was on the point of being arrested and charged with fraud, wouldn't involve me in any way when the case came to trial. However, in the meantime, he suffered a heart attack and died; and, as I'm quite sure you're already very well aware, the whole matter, due to lack of evidence, was then hushed up to avoid a loss of public faith in building societies generally and a rush by depositors up and down the country to withdraw their savings."

He made a small, dispirited gesture with his hand. "You know, of course, that I went up to Cynthia's room late on Friday night to talk to her. Nelson . . . if that's the fellow's name—the retired naval officer—saw me; or I'm fairly sure he did; and I knew it'd only be a matter of time before you found that out and tied it in with the building society fraud; but I'd hoped, for Kath's—my wife's—sake that you'd find out who'd killed Cynthia before it went that far."

Rhys-Williams, who was standing by the fireplace, sighed to himself and gazed despondently out of the window at the lawned square beyond. He had been wondering how long it would be before Sexton got round to his wife. Sexton's kind always had an excuse for their own shortcomings and stupidity, someone on whom they could lay some if not all the blame and charge with being the cause of their predicament.

Sexton went on, "I was telling the truth about what happened when Cynthia phoned down to reception on Friday night; she really had rung off by the time I'd got out there." He covered his face with his hands, left them there for a moment, then rubbed his fingertips into his eyes leaving them red and bleary. "God, if only I'd turned right round and gone straight back to the Wellington Room. None of this would've happened. But I was curious." He sighed, slumped back in the chair, and closed his eyes. "Was it really only that, curiosity? Or did I hope that there was still a chance for us?" He looked directly at Walsh. His gaze never wavered; his voice was stready. "I loved that woman, really loved her. She was a bitch: cruel, vicious; but—God knows why!—I loved her. I'd have done almost anything for her; given her anything. She had only to ask."

"But she didn't ask; she threatened to blackmail you."

Sexton frowned. "She must've been mad. No, perhaps that's too strong a word for it. Temporarily unbalanced. When I think back now over our conversation that night, I wonder if I didn't imagine it all."

"How much did she want?"

Sexton gave Walsh an odd look. "Money, you mean?"

"That's what it's usually all about, isn't it? Blackmail?"

"Cynthia didn't want money from me." Sexton laughed that Walsh should think she had. "She had some crazy notion that I could fix the competition—the one that was held yesterday afternoon. Cynthia and I were on the panel of judges—there were four of us altogether—and she had made up her mind how they, the other two—her brother and Headley, our president—were going to vote, and she wanted me to vote with her and persuade Headley to change his mind."

Walsh's bemused gaze brought a slow smile to Sexton's lips. "I told you there was something strange about her; she wasn't thinking straight. She was quite worked up about it, the competition. I never did fully understand what was behind it all . . . some disagreement she and her brother were having over Alison Crosby, the young woman who won. Cynthia was always very jealous of Nigel. Possessive. We've already gone into what people used to say about them—" he frowned "—so I'd rather not dwell on it, if you wouldn't mind. Anyway, I told her it wasn't on —that sort of thing has never been right as far as I'm concerned; and if she'd been in her right mind, she would've known better than to think she could get me to change my stand. Besides, the competition was too small and intimate to cover up something like that; the audience would've caught on and wouldn't have stood for it, particularly if the girl had turned in the best performance—which, in the event, is what actually happened. I tried to make Cynthia see that, but she got quite hysterical and wouldn't listen to me. I began to get alarmed. I'd never seen her that way before—worked up, yes, but always reasonably in control. I told her to get a hold of herself and that if she calmed down and thought things over quietly and sensibly, she'd see that there was nothing I could do to stop that girl from winning the competition.

"By this time I was getting pretty worked up myself, and while I know it was an idiotic thing to say in the circumstances, I said that if this was what she really wanted, then there was only one way to go about it, and that was to find some means of preventing Alison Crosby from getting on stage on Sunday. Naturally, when the rumour went around the next day that one of the conventioneers, a woman, had fallen to her death from the cabin lift in mysterious circumstances, I thought it was Alison and that Cynthia was behind it—she'd taken me literally at my word!

"I knew Cynthia was going for a ride up the mountain on Saturday morning: I was supposed to meet her at the summit at ten-thirty with my decision about the girl. I told her it wouldn't make any difference, my answer would be exactly the same; but she insisted that I was to be there or else, and right up until the last minute, I fully intended to keep my appointment with her. I hadn't changed my mind about the competition, but I thought that I could perhaps talk some sense into her. However, when the time actually came for me to leave to go and meet her, I suddenly decided against it and went for a walk on the beach instead. I knew it was useless trying to talk to her in her present frame of mind; it would've probably only made matters worse; and as for her threat to expose me . . . well, that was up to her. It wouldn't have been the first time someone had pointed the finger of suspicion at me. She had no proof; it would've been her word against mine."

Sexton frowned at the interruption as the telephone pealed insistently. Rhys-Williams stepped swiftly forward and silenced it on the second ring. He said a few words, then covered the mouthpiece with his left hand and turned to Walsh. "It's that insurance investigator, Sayer, sir. He'd like a word with you."

"Take care of it please, Sergeant," said Walsh with an annoyed frown. He was still smarting over one or two things Sayer had said to him yesterday concerning the handling of his interview with the clairvoyante. "Somewhere else, if you don't mind. Find out what the problem is and tell Sayer I'll call him back later."

"He's here, sir. In the hotel."

Walsh looked away and said sharply, "See to it, will you?"

Rhys-Williams removed his hand from the mouthpiece and said that someone would be right out. He was back almost immediately. "I'm sorry, sir," he began. "Sayer insists that he must see you personally right away. He's with that fortune teller." The sergeant raised his eyebrows a little at the angry look Walsh gave him. "The lady has an envelope with her, sir. . . ."

Rhys-Williams, knowing Walsh's theory about the probable

present whereabouts of the envelope missing from Cynthia Play-ford's shoulder bag, was tempted to add, "You know, the one the goat didn't eat," but thought better of it. Walsh wasn't in the mood.

CHAPTER 21

Sayer and the clairvoyante were waiting in the small lounge off reception. As the Chief Inspector approached, they rose. The clairvoyante was the first to speak.

"Good morning, Chief Inspector. Thank you for seeing us so promptly. I believe you've been looking for this—"

She handed him a long brown envelope. Along the top left-hand corner, in chunky black letters, was the pertinent information: PRINTED MATTER ONLY. There was no name and address on the front of it. He turned it over. A small white self-adhesive label on the flap bore the name and address of C. L. Playford, 94 The Grove, Broadstairs, Kent.

Walsh looked up questioningly at the clairvoyante.

"I'm sorry I've taken so long to come forward with it," she said, "but up until a short while ago, when Mr. Sayer and I met and I discussed its contents with him, I had no idea the police were looking for it. As I've already explained to Mr. Sayer, Cynthia Playford gave it to me on Saturday morning. Over there in reception," she added, indicating with her right hand. "I had just arrived—this would've been somewhere around nine-thirty—and she was on her way out. I'd previously discussed our brief meeting in reception that morning with Mr. Sayer; and as I told him then, Cynthia was in a distressed state and frankly not making much sense. At least, that was how it seemed at the time. But now that I've had a chance to go through the papers in the envelope, I can begin to understand what she was talking about. Broadly speaking, when Cynthia handed me the envelope—she'd taken it from her shoulder bag where she said it was taking up too much room and she wanted to be rid of it—I knew what it contained . . . photocopies of old documents she had uncovered and notes she'd made while researching an obscure Victorian novelist, one of the earliest exponents of the crime-detective novel; and this was why I merely put the envelope away in my luggage without looking inside it straightaway. Her cryptic comment as she handed me the envelope—I can't remember her exact words, but she said something to the effect that I would find the papers specially interesting; a sick joke, I clearly remember her saying; and that we would discuss them over lunch—I assumed related to my late mother's association with the Victorian novelist.

"You see, Chief Inspector; this was why Cynthia Playford first got in touch with me. Not because I'm a clairvoyante, nor because she had need of the help of one—all that came later. Cynthia originally contacted me because my mother was a world famous Edwardian operatic star, though not at the time of her friendship with the novelist I mentioned. My mother was only a girl of about seventeen then; the daughter of an Italian count who had disowned and disinherited her when she ran away from home to pursue a career in the theatre. Amanda Beddoes, the Victorian novelist I referred to, found my mother in a distressed state, living in appalling conditions in the East End of London and took her under her wing. . . ."

"Yes, yes," said Walsh impatiently. "All very interesting, I'm sure. But what has all this got to do with Cynthia Playford's murder?"

"Everything, Griffith," said Sayer soberly. "Mrs. Charles and I believe Cynthia Playford was murdered because of what she uncovered while researching into the life of Amanda Beddoes."

The clairvoyante said, "That envelope contains months of painstaking research. It took me many hours to go through all the papers and reach the conclusions I have about Cynthia Playford's death; and it will likewise take you as long to go through them. However, if you wish, I can give you a brief résumé—"

"Not here," said Walsh quickly. They had begun to draw one or two curious stares. "Let's go outside and talk."

Lightly touching her left elbow, and with Sayer close on their heels, Walsh guided the clairvoyante across the lounge into reception, then through the revolving door to the street. Abruptly, Walsh pulled her sharply back and then drew her quickly to one side clear of the two ambulance men who had suddenly swooped on them from out of nowhere, the stretcher they bore between them aimed at the single swing door to the left of the revolving one like a battering ram. With the country's ambulance service now all but completely paralysed by a long-standing industrial dispute, it stood to reason that the call had to be an emergency of the gravest kind. Walsh watched the two men over his shoulder for a moment before glancing thoughtfully at the gleaming new ambulance parked on his right, almost completely blocking the forecourt; then, in response to the questioning look in the clairvoyante's eye, he nodded that he was ready to continue.

Stepping down from the columned entrance porch, the clairvoyante, flanked on either side by Walsh and Sayer, crossed the forecourt and strolled for some minutes in silence through wintry sunshine and a brisk northeasterly wind to the far side of the square where there was a vacant bench.

Walsh seated himself on the clairvoyante's right; then folding his arms, he gazed back across the square at the imposing Victorian facade of the hotel. From where he sat, it was impossible to say what had become of the ambulance, whether it had gone. The envelope was tucked under his right arm, its bulky contents pricking his side like a bad conscience. He had glanced only once at Sayer, whose facial expression had given very little away —only that Walsh had made a damned fool of himself, as Sayer had predicted.

"Go on about this obscure Victorian novelist," said Walsh dispiritedly.

"It all began," the clairvoyante responded, "approximately twelve months ago with a letter Cynthia received from an American writer who was preparing a foreword to an American reprint of one of the novelist's books, requesting her to try and get him the date of the novelist's birth, which had always been something of a mystery in itself. The date of the novelist's death is widely known—one can get it from any reference library—but there's no record anywhere of her birth date (it's just shown with what few details there are in the records on her as being eighteen hundred and blank); and the American writer's editor rather wanted it included, if possible, in the foreword to the reprint.

"To begin with, Cynthia came up against the same brick wall that had blocked all the other researchers before her when they'd tried to find the records of the novelist's birth—incidentally, she wrote only eight novels in all; she was better known, according to her obituary in *The Times*, for her work in the women's suffrage movement and for her tireless campaigning for the improvement of the female's lot generally, although she herself was extremely happily married and absolutely devoted to her husband, an ex-naval officer. All the male members of her husband's family were high-ranking naval officers who distinguished themselves in one way or another in battle. Her own husband received a medal at the end of the Chinese War in 1858—"

Mrs. Charles paused at the sharp turn of Walsh's head. "Yes, Chief Inspector," she said quietly, anticipating the question she knew would follow the steady look he was levelling at her. "You heard me correctly. Naval officers. Every last one of them."

Walsh nodded, watched the leisurely approach of an ambulance—presumably the one which had been waiting outside the hotel—his head turning slowly as he followed its progress around the square and out of sight. Frowning slightly, he indicated that he wished the clairvoyante to continue.

"The sick joke Cynthia referred to when we spoke briefly in reception on Saturday morning, and her reason for saying that I'd be specially interested were not directly concerned with my mother's association with Amanda Beddoes, as I'd naturally imagined, but with my increasing involvement over the past few years in unsolved murder cases. Amanda Beddoes, a writer of murder mysteries, became herself one of the victims of a double-murder plot even more bizarre than anything she ever wrote. An extremely sick joke, admittedly, but not without its fascination—that sort of situation. All the murders in her books were solved—by a female law clerk-*cum*-private detective, very emancipated naturally and as often as not chained to railings in support of women's suffrage when not solving crimes!—whereas Amanda Beddoes' own murder wasn't even detected, let alone solved."

Mrs. Charles nodded in response to the quick glance Walsh gave her. "I'm quite sure that when you go through those papers, you'll agree with Mr. Sayer and me—and Cynthia Playford—that there's a very good possibility that the novelist and her husband were the victims of the perfect crime."

She paused and smiled at the way Walsh was looking at her. "Cynthia Playford was a highly competent professional researcher, Chief Inspector—someone like you, who only deals in hard facts. The novelist and her husband died in 1912, within eight days of one another, her first then him. Sad but not uncommon—a sociological-psychological phenomenon of elderly devoted couples, as I believe I've heard the psychologists refer to it. However, when one examines the documents carefully, the copies of the death certificates in particular, a very different picture begins to emerge.

"In both instances the name of the informant on the death certificates is the same, a nephew; and he was also the doctor in attendance. And do you know where the murderer—the doctor-nephew—made his mistake? The novelist and her husband were childless; and the husband's nephew, their doctor, inherited a fortune as a result of their deaths—" the clairvoyante put in with a quick frown "—well over a million pounds, Cynthia put the figure at . . . that's at today's values, though he didn't live long to enjoy his ill-gotten gains; he was killed while on active service with the Royal Navy in 1917. . . . He made a mistake in his aunt's age on her death certificate; that's why no one was ever able to trace any record of her birth—until Cynthia came along, that is. He thought his aunt was sixty-eight when she died; and sixty-eight deducted from 1912, the year of death, gave Cynthia (and all the others researchers before her) 1844 as being the year of her birth.

"But Cynthia—and everyone else who'd looked, obviously—could find no trace of the novelist, whose maiden name was Portman, in the records either for that year, 1844, or during the two or three years at either side of it. Then to complicate matters even further, Cynthia discovered that at around that time—the early 1840's—people were still very suspicious of a newfangled law, which came into being in 1837, requiring that all births should be registered; and that as a result of this, many births went unregistered. No doubt the other researchers made the self-same discovery, assumed that the novelist was amongst these casualties of parental ignorance, and gave up the search.

"Cynthia, however, thought it most unlikely that the Portman family—the novelist's father was a well-to-do lawyer—would've been scared off by the new law, so she went back to the beginning and started all over again. Only this time she worked on the premise that since the informant of the novelist's death wasn't her husband but his nephew, the age at the time of death given on her death certificate was wildly inaccurate; and that perhaps by reason of vanity, the novelist had deliberately kept her age down and told the nephew—who was also her doctor, you'll remember, and should've therefore known her correct age—that she was a much younger woman than she really was. Six years younger, in point of fact. She was really seventy-four when she died, not sixty-eight, and was born, Cynthia eventually discovered, in 1838. And from that one little slip of his. . . ."

The words beat loudly against Walsh's eardrums. He listened in silence, haunted by visions of Mrs. Belson asking his permission to return to London with her sick husband. . . . *A man who can give orders, a man who can take them and not ask questions* —that was the broad outline of the character profile which Eli Jones, the ticket seller for the Great Mountain cabin lift, had drawn after briefly studying the hand of the man who had got into the cabin with Cynthia Playford. An observation which could have applied equally well to Frank Sexton as chairman of the board, but was rather better suited to Captain James Belson, R.N. (Retired). Except that Belson wasn't his real name. He had kept the *B*, the initial of his real surname, as most people generally do when assuming a false identity; and then, with another high-ranking naval officer in mind, Vice Admiral Lord Nelson, he had changed his name from Beddoes to Belson. Even Frank Sexton, not so many minutes ago, had made a slip, through not being overly familiar with the man, and referred to him as "Nelson."

"Captain James Beddoes," Walsh morosely interrupted the clairvoyante at length. "I presume there's a family tree of some description amongst the papers—"

Without saying a word, Mrs. Charles retrieved the envelope and sorted quickly through its contents, finally withdrawing a closely typewritten sheet of white flimsy, partway down which and underlined twice in red ink was the name of the Victorian suffragette and crime novelist, Amanda Vanessa Beddoes.

Walsh went on in a distant voice, "He's now probably somewhere in his late fifties; and I understand that he got married during the first few weeks of the Second World War."

Mrs. Charles, who had long since drawn the same conclusion that Walsh had about Belson, scanned the information given on James Alph Beddoes, only son of Dr. and Mrs. Charles Alph Beddoes, did some quick mental arithmetic, and then shook her head. "No, you're wrong on both counts. He's sixty-three; and he married one Abigail Vickers at Valetta, Malta, on July 10, 1938—just over a year before the outbreak of war. He was a lieutenant then. His father was—" The clairvoyante looked up with a sudden frown when Walsh laughed softly. "Have I said something funny?" she asked.

He shook his head. "It was just that bit about Malta. I was merely thinking what incredibly good liars some people are."

Mrs. Charles recalled what Mrs. Belson had told her about Malta. It had been her reason for consulting the clairvoyante— not really a lie, more of a half-truth that she and her husband contemplated retiring to the sunny Mediterranean island; but sadly, the whole truth when she had spoken of their happiness there early in their marriage.

Rising, Walsh said, "I think I've heard enough for now. We'd better be getting back. There's someone I really ought to put out of his misery. . . ."

CHAPTER 22

"What happened?"

Kath Sexton left the open suitcases and the miscellany of male and female clothing and other smaller personal belongings which lay scattered across the bedspread waiting to be packed and moved quickly round the bed. She paused at the foot of it, her dark eyes searching her husband's face anxiously.

"I'm not really sure," he replied thoughtfully. "One minute he looked all set to arrest me and the next. . . ." He paused, frowned. "The fortune teller—Madame Herrmann—and somebody by the name of Sayer suddenly turned up wanting to see him, and he disappeared for about half an hour. Then, when he came back, he just asked me one or two more questions and then he said I could go; he'd want a full statement from me later on, he said—before we left—but that was all for the moment. Actually thanked me for all my help." He shrugged irritably. "The man has to be some kind of idiot!"

"What did he want to know?"

"Just if I'd seen anyone on Cynthia's floor when I went up to see her on Friday night." He hesitated, frowning again. "I guess you've known all along about that—that I did go up there . . . I was lying."

Kath brushed aside his confession. "Did you see anyone?" His quick nod made her heart lurch sickeningly. Her knees weak and shaky, she moved unsteadily over to the dressing table where she groped absentmindedly for her hairbrush. Then she sat down on a clear space near the foot of the bed on which she had been doing the packing. This was something she hadn't expected, that Frank had seen the night porter up there that night. And now, if he'd admitted seeing him to the police and they were notified, as inevitably they would be, that he'd gone missing—or word got round that he hadn't turned up for his shift, whichever was the sooner—Frank was bound to be implicated in his disappearance. Odd, though, she thought with an anxious frown, that the porter hadn't said anything to her about Frank's having seen him. . . .

"You've gone very quiet all of a sudden," Sexton observed. "What's wrong?"

"Nothing. I've just got a bit of a headache, that's all." She paused, tried to look and sound casual. "What did the police have to say about that . . . when you told them you had seen someone?"

"Very little, really. He'd obviously told them he'd seen me in reception while he was arranging for some sandwiches to be sent up to his wife."

She gave him a puzzled look. "Whose wife? Who are you talking about?"

"The heavy breather. Belson."

"Belson?" she echoed numbly. For the moment her mind was so confused she couldn't think straight. Who the hell was he? Oh, yes. . . . "The retired sea captain—that was who you saw?" she asked in a bewildered voice.

"Yes. Who else did you think?"

She shook her head and looked down quickly at the hand clutching the hairbrush. "No one, of course. I didn't even know for sure that you'd gone up to Cynthia's room until you just admitted it to me."

"Belson was hanging about out in the corridor. I thought he'd had to pause to catch his breath. You've spoken to him; you know how breathless he's inclined to be."

The fingers of Kath's left hand dug deep into the pile of the bedspread. She spoke haltingly. "Could he have overheard anything, do you think?"

"Of what Cynthia and I had been talking about?" He shook his head. "I doubt it. He wasn't standing right outside the door."

She looked up at him and sighed. "Thank heaven for that."

"You might be a little premature there."

She frowned. "What do you mean?"

"I've an idea he might've heard what Cynthia said to me as I was coming out of her room and about to leave. She was pretty hysterical, talking shrilly, and the door was wide open—only for a few seconds, mind you—but he'd have to be deaf as a post not to have heard what she said. In which case," he sighed heavily, "he'll be able to confirm what I've just told them, the police . . . that Cynthia and I had arranged to meet at the summit of Great Mountain on Saturday morning. That's if he hasn't got in before me, and I expect he has; the police are past masters at never letting their right hand know what the left's doing; so you can bet they already knew all about it from him and were just waiting to see what I'd say. I stepped back quickly the moment I spotted him in the corridor and closed the door again; but I'm almost sure he saw me because of the way he suddenly got a move on, though it might've been the lift that galvanized him into action. That came to a stop at practically the same instant . . . his sandwiches coming up, I suppose. I put up with Cynthia's hectoring for another five or so minutes—until I thought the coast was clear —and then I left. Belson had gone by this time."

Kath was as white as a sheet. "Oh God, Frank," she murmured. "I thought it was going to be all right." Her voice quickened. "Do you know anything about them, the Belsons—where they live?"

"No, you've had more to say to them than I have. Why?"

"I thought—" Kath hesitated, chewed her bottom lip for a moment. "Maybe we could talk to them." She dropped the hairbrush on the bed and crossed quickly to the telephone. "The Toomeys," she said, picking up the receiver and holding it to her ear. "That peculiar-looking couple who were always with the Belsons. . . . Maybe they'll have their address. I overheard Mrs. Belson telling Mrs. Toomey at breakfast this morning that she and her husband were hoping to leave today. I think—" she frowned "—I heard Mrs. Belson say that her husband wasn't feeling too well."

The protest on Sexton's lips was drowned out by her voice asking if Mr. and Mrs. Toomey were still guests. Apparently they weren't; they had checked out at midmorning. Then, before Sexton could express his relief at this piece of news, Kath was inquiring about the Belsons. They had checked out too, hadn't they?

Whatever the switchboard operator's response, it had an electrifying effect on Kath. Without a word, she dropped the receiver and flew to the door.

Her husband made a successful grab for her arm as she was about to dash past him. "You're overreacting a bit, aren't you?" he said with a frown. "Leave it alone, Kath. It's out of our hands now."

She covered the hand on her arm with hers and looked steadily into his eyes. "Trust me, Frank," she said, her voice heavy with emotion. She squeezed his hand a little. "I know what I'm doing; just leave everything to me."

He shook his head and withdrew his hand from under hers. "I still say you're overreacting. For all either of us knows, Belson mightn't have heard a thing; he mightn't have even seen me."

"That's what I intend to find out," she said. "I won't be long."

He closed the door behind her. Then, shaking his head again, he crossed to the bed with the suitcases on it, gazed thoughtfully at it for a moment, and then went on with the half-finished packing.

Somehow Walsh did not expect good news. He had heard all about Belson, that he had collapsed in reception moments after settling his bill and had had to be assisted back to his room. The doctor and Walsh passed one another as Walsh got out of the lift at the second floor. The doctor was leaving. They exchanged abrupt nods, neither man saying anything.

Walsh went up the corridor, passing the room which Cynthia Playford had occupied during her brief stay at the hotel, then moving along another, shorter one.

Mrs. Belson opened the door. There was no anxiety or distress in her expression, in the way her eyes searched his, only a quiet acceptance of what she had known all along was inevitable.

"May I?" he asked. Then, after a tiny pause: "Mrs. Beddoes."

She looked steadily at him, then lowered her gaze submissively and moved aside for him to pass. She seemed reluctant to turn and face him, and addressed the first of her remarks to the closed door.

"James has gone," she said quietly. "About half an hour ago. In an ambulance. They've taken him to the local hospital. The doctor has just left."

Walsh was coming away from Abigail and James Beddoes's room as the lift doors opened and Kath Sexton stepped out.

She gave a start and hesitated when she saw him appear. "Oh," she said. Then a second time, nonplussed: *"Oh!"* she said. Colour flooded her pale face until her cheeks burned a bright red. She looked round at the waiting lift as if in two minds whether or not to make a run for it. Then, looking back at Walsh, her eyelids fluttering under his quizzical gaze: "I—I was just going to have a word with Cap—I mean, *Mrs.* Belson."

Walsh considered her fiery complexion for a moment before saying, "I'm afraid you're a little too late for that . . . That's if," he went on after a slight pause, "you were right the first time and it was the captain you were wanting."

She glanced quickly round him as if doubting his word and expecting to see the captain bringing up the rear. "They've left?"

"No, only Captain—" he hesitated "—Belson. He's dead, I'm sorry to have to say."

Kath stared at him. Her mouth opened as if she were about to say something, then she snapped it firmly shut. She turned abruptly away and Walsh stepped after her into the lift. "Up or down?" he inquired. "I'm going down."

"Down will do," she replied absently. The lift doors closed with a swish and a thud. Her mind was in a turmoil. *God, now what?* She looked at Walsh. "Were you . . . did you speak to Captain Belson before he died?"

"No, I'm afraid I was too late too."

"Oh," she said in a small voice.

The lift gave a sudden lurch, throwing them both momentarily a little off-balance, juddered, then stopped. The doors parted and Walsh stood back to allow her to pass. He was puzzled by the look in her eyes, the covert glance she gave him. She seemed relieved—no, *pleased*—about something . . . That Belson (Beddoes) had died before he could speak to him? Why should that please her?

Walsh remained standing in the lift and watched her cross to the reception desk; then, as he moved to follow her, he heard her ask the girl to make up her bill and say that she and her husband would be checking out sometime later that day. There was a lilt to her voice and, when she turned away from the desk, a lightness in her step, something totally carefree and lighthearted in the way she swung her arms. This was a completely different woman he was seeing, sure and confident of herself, nothing like the nervous, diffident person who had stepped out of the lift at the second floor less than five minutes ago and spoken to him.

He gazed pensively at her as she got back into the lift, then shook himself a little and walked off briskly in the direction of the Marlborough Room.

Kath swiftly closed the door and fell back against it with a quick laugh. Then she realised: the room was empty, the luggage gone. Only a few small items remained on the dressing table: her cosmetics, the hairbrush, a box of Kleenex, and in the bathroom (she took a hurried look in there) the wet pack—things she usually packed at the very last moment into the zippered airline bag which was standing on the floor near the dressing-table stool.

Blood rushed to her head and pounded in her temples. She swung about and flung open the door, then stopped dead in her tracks. Her husband was standing in the corridor just outside the door. His face, under the tan, was grey; the hand that reached out to her, trembling.

There was a peculiar abrasiveness to his voice, a kind of fear, when he said, "I've just been out to the garage with the luggage."

She turned aside, drawing him into the room with her, then quickly closed the door. "It's all right, Frank," she said soothingly. "Here, sit down." She drew him over to one of the beds and gently forced him down onto it. "I've been meaning to talk to you—"

He looked up at her protestingly. "Kath, *listen* . . . you don't seem to understand."

She put an arm round his shoulders and patted him comfortingly. "*Ssh, ssh*—I know, I know," she crooned. "I understand perfectly, my darling. You mustn't worry about anything. I've got it all worked out; I know now exactly what we're going to do. It's going to be all right. You must believe that, Frank." She paused and frowned at him. "Why did you take the luggage down to the car so early? I thought you said you still had another statement to make to the police?"

"Yes, yes—" he made an impatient gesture with his hand "—later, before we leave. I just thought I'd save a bit of time, that's all." He twisted himself free of her hold and looked at her urgently. "Kath, listen to me for a moment. The night porter, the midget—you remember him, the one with the humped back. He's—"

"*Ssh*," she whispered lovingly. "Be quiet, my darling. It had to be done. He was the only one who could really harm you. He was outside the door of Cynthia's room on Friday night; he heard her threaten you." She knelt on the floor before him. "Captain Belson is dead, Frank. A heart attack, I suppose—" she shrugged. "I can't say he'd looked well all weekend. He died before the police had time to speak to him again." She gazed up into his face and her voice took on an excited urgency. "Did you hear what I said, Frank? *Belson is dead!*"

Sexton was shaking his head distractedly. In God's name, what was wrong with the woman? She hadn't heard a word he'd said. "Kath, you're not listening to me. Forget about Belson. It's the night porter I'm talking about."

She laid her head on his knee. "He knew you killed Cynthia, Frank. He could've got you sent to prison for a very long time. I couldn't bear that, Frank; I won't let them take you away from me."

He stared down at her dark head. This was a nightmare. He was going mad!

"Kath," he said desperately. "Please try to understand. *I didn't kill Cynthia.*"

"Yes, dear." She was crooning again, as one might to a small, much-loved child whose vilest misdemeanour would anyway always find forgiveness and understanding in the eyes of its doting mother. "I know, dear. We won't talk about it any more, will we?"

CHAPTER 23

The holiday weekend seemed a long way in the past to the detective sergeant even though this was only the following Thursday.

Walsh had completed his investigations and seemed happy enough—as happy as one could ever hope to be in the circumstances. He had been discussing the Playford case with the Chief Constable for the past hour, and Rhys-Williams was expecting him back at any minute. As far as possible, the near monosyllabic Chief Constable strenuously avoided lengthy discussions, especially ones centred largely on conjecture. And the evidence against Captain James Beddoes, R.N. (Retired), was slight in the extreme, though there was no doubt in the sergeant's mind that Beddoes had killed Cynthia Playford, even if he did feel aggrieved that the man had died before Walsh could question him again.

Rhys-Williams glanced at the electric wall clock; debated whether he would slip away to The Swan for a pint and a bite to eat. He decided to wait. Walsh might be put out if he went off to lunch without him, especially after Walsh had said he was buying today. The Chief Constable would turn him out soon, anyway. Was bound to.

Another twenty minutes elapsed before Walsh finally returned to his office.

"Well," said Rhys-Williams as the Chief Inspector came through the door. "What did God have to say about your theory?"

"It's more than a theory, lad," said Walsh pleasantly. "You know as well as I do that the cabin-lift mechanic has positively identified Beddoes as being the man he loaded into the cabin with Cynthia Playford that morning."

"For what that's worth," the sergeant said disgruntledly. "That particular party's—Will Llewellyn's—testimony. Not that it matters much now . . . with Beddoes snuffing it."

Walsh smiled. "Never mind, lad. You win some, you lose some."

"We certainly lost this one. Beddoes couldn't have picked better timing for making his exit."

Walsh, who had perched himself casually on the edge of his desk, nodded. "Yes, poor devil."

Rhys-Williams stared at him. "Poor devil? Any minute now you'll be telling me he made the supreme sacrifice and be putting his name forward for some kind of medal for doing what he did!"

Walsh grinned at his subordinate's indignation. "He was the only one, y'know, the only Beddoes who never distinguished himself in battle. No awards for bravery, or special citations; no mention in despatches. And the way I see it, that's the nut and bolt of the whole issue. I think Beddoes did make the supreme sacrifice, not for his country—or only in a very indirect way—but for all the male Beddoeses who'd gone before him who had so distinguished themselves in the service of their country and whose honourable and dignified memory had become threatened by a literary researcher who'd dug a little too deeply and unearthed the still mouldering family skeleton. He didn't care for himself, lad; after reading up on the quite outstanding role his ancestors played in British naval history, I'm convinced of that. One can imagine how a man like him, with his background, would feel. . . . The curse of the Beddoeses, you might say, had finally come home to roost."

Walsh was quiet for a moment, thinking about what he had said. Then, eyebrows raised: "Do you know who it was who wrote that about curses and young chickens coming home to roost? Robert Southey—Nelson's biographer—in *The Curse of Kehama*. Curious that, I thought . . . the Beddoeses always having been naval officers too and falling foul of that particular writer's prediction. All the more so since Beddoes basically took Nelson's name for a pseudonym."

"You don't seriously think Beddoes' father really did do away with—who was it . . . Beddoes' aunt?—great-aunt," Rhys-Williams corrected himself, "and her husband a few days later so as to inherit their money? Surely that was only Cynthia Playford's imagination running away with her."

"And James Beddoes? He had problems with an overworked imagination too? Cynthia Playford and Beddoes *both* imagined the same thing?" Walsh shook his head. "I'm not suggesting for one moment that Beddoes knew for sure that his father was a murderer—in fact I think it highly unlikely that he knew any more about the allegation concerning his father than the rest of the Beddoes family did. But for him to feel so threatened by Cynthia Playford's interest in his great-aunt that he was driven to take the step he did, then he had to have had more than just a faint suspicion that what his aunts and uncles and near and distant cousins had always whispered behind his back might've actually been true and his father had committed murder as they alleged."

Walsh left the edge of his desk and went round to the chair and sat down. "Shall I tell you how I really see it, lad?" he said, folding his arms across his chest.

"What are we talking about? The if-and-maybe murder of the great-aunt and uncle, or Cynthia Playford's murder?"

"We'll start with the great-aunt's. There's a fifty-fifty chance that she, at least, was murdered." He smiled at the look Rhys-Williams shot at him. "Come on, lad, the graveyards are full of them—undetected murder victims . . . eccentric Amanda Vanessa Beddoeses with more money than is good for their health, especially when they start doling it out, as she did, to East End prostitutes and their illegitimate offspring, and the heir apparent to the Beddoes family fortune looks in real danger of dipping out altogether if he doesn't soon take a firm stand in matters. The papers relating to Amanda Beddoes' exact financial involvement with the women's suffrage movement were destroyed during the Blitz—"

"Fact?" the sergeant interrupted dryly. "Or the fiction the Beddoes family would like to have you believe?"

"No, I've checked on it. Those particular records really did go up in smoke during the war. However, Amanda Beddoes' obituary in *The Times* makes it pretty plain that she was definitely fairly heavily committed financially to the movement, and that the battle she without a doubt personally waged for the improvement of the lot of the female underdog—which certainly would appear to have gathered considerable momentum during the last few years of her life—wasn't merely confined to fiery speeches from the campaign platform. Where the speculation comes in is over what the ex–daughter-in-law of the retired naval attaché—Sir Archibald Beddoes—told me yesterday of the family gossip she'd heard about James Beddoes's father."

"The divorcée?" Rhys-Williams, who had accompanied Walsh to London the previous day to interview various members of the Beddoes family, made a face. "That old battle-axe was so embittered about her ex–in-laws and the Beddoes family generally that she'd have told you anything she thought you wanted to hear."

"Probably. But what she said could fit, that's if—" Walsh smiled faintly "—you wanted it to fit . . . Amanda Beddoes dropping hints shortly before she died that she was contemplating altering her will and leaving everything to underprivileged women and children instead of to her husband's nephew. Though that was not strictly correct, the bit about the nephew inheriting outright—the ex–daughter-in-law had got her facts muddled there. Amanda Beddoes' will, as it stood (and this was the will which was eventually proved), was more complicated than that; and the only way the nephew—James Beddoes' father —would've benefited under it would've been if her husband were to predecease her, or die within a month of her death. Hence the need, one would suppose—" the Chief Inspector smiled again "—for the nephew to eliminate her husband with such indecent haste—and by no means is it terribly likely that he did any such thing, not in the uncle's case—roughly a week after she died. And as for the long period of chronic diarrhoea which the ex–daughter-in-law claims the Beddoes family put down to arsenical poisoning. . . ." Walsh's pursed lips gave Rhys-Williams rise to wonder, and not for the first time since the Chief Inspector had begun talking, if he weren't deliberately making fun of him. "Very popular at the time, lad. For doing away with the odd unwanted relative or two. Right in fashion. And who better to get away with it than her doctor?"

"Beddoes' father really was her doctor?"

Walsh nodded. "He was later killed while serving as a surgeon with the Royal Navy during the closing stages of the First World War, when James Beddoes, his son, was only a baby. I doubt if Beddoes ever knew him."

"And the Beddoes fortune his father inherited after he'd supposedly surmounted the two obstacles to his attaining it? Where did that finish up?"

"Not in James Beddoes' pocket. Cynthia Playford discovered that. His mother was ill advised over her financial affairs—this was after Beddoes' father was killed—and within ten years there was nothing left and Beddoes and his mother were reduced to living off family charity."

"Seems odd to me . . . that the Beddoeses are supposed to have always had their suspicions about the real cause of the great-aunt's death and yet no one ever did anything about it."

"Ah, but they did do something about it, lad—if we're to believe what the retired naval attaché's ex–daughter-in-law told me. They admitted their fears to one another—held a family conference, so to speak—and unanimously decided to let sleeping dogs lie, as it were. No doubt none of them was too crazy about the idea of poor old Amanda and (possibly) her husband having been done away with so summarily; but one can see why it'd be infinitely preferable from their point of view that it should remain nothing more than a suspicion within the immediate family circle. Think about it, imagine the humiliation and disgrace of the world at large knowing that one of their undeniably distinguished number had committed murder. Not to mention having it become common knowledge that the motive for the first crime, at least—Amanda Beddoes' murder—had resulted (in their opinion) from what they anyway considered—as the ex–daughter-in-law was so anxious to have me understand—was a highly eccentric and somewhat unbalanced whim to leave a vast amount of money to common prostitutes and their bastards. Remember, this is Edwardian England we're talking about, lad—" Walsh broke off. From where he was sitting, he had an uninterrupted view of the car park to the front of the main entrance to the Plaid-yro-Wyth Constabulary. David Sayer had just driven up. The clairvoyante was with him.

"We're about to have visitors," said Walsh. "Nip out to the front desk and wheel 'em in, will you?"

Walsh got to his feet, smiling, as the clairvoyante and Sayer were ushered into his office by the sergeant. Shaking hands with the clairvoyante, he said, "It was good of you . . . er, Madame, to remain in Plaid-yro-Wyth for a few extra days until we had everything more or less sorted out."

Rhys-Williams brought two chairs up to the Chief Inspector's desk, and Mrs. Charles and Sayer sat down.

"Well, what d'you think?" asked Sayer. "Was Cynthia Playford blackmailing him—Beddoes?"

"Mrs. Beddoes says not and there's no evidence of it."

"So what was in it for her—for Cynthia Playford, that is?" asked Sayer.

Walsh shook his head. "Anyone's guess. Kicks, probably. A woman of her character would find the whole thing vastly amusing—it's certainly the impression I gained from the notes she slipped in with the papers connected with her research on Amanda Beddoes which she passed on to you, Madame," Walsh said to the clairvoyante. "I think it appealed to her somewhat macabre sense of humour that Amanda Beddoes, a one-time crime-fiction writer, had herself possibly finished up the victim of the sort of crime she used to write about. A woman like

Cynthia Playford, totally self-centred and, more to the point, malicious and vindictive with it, wouldn't begin to understand how Beddoes must've felt or even care how distressed he obviously was over her obsessive interest in his family."

"Well, no one can say he didn't sort her out!" Rhys-Williams interpolated.

CHAPTER 24

Walsh considered his subordinate's remark. Then, thoughtfully: "I think he tried less drastic measures first; and I'm not entirely convinced that it was cold-blooded, premeditated murder. Nobody knows—and Mrs. Beddoes certainly isn't saying—what transpired between Beddoes and Cynthia Playford as they rode up Great Mountain on the cabin lift last Saturday morning; but what happened up there could've been an accident."

Rhys-Williams was looking at Walsh as if he had gone mad; but the clairvoyante, the Chief Inspector covertly noted—if the look in her eyes was anything to go by—was in full agreement with him.

The sergeant said, "After Beddoes had stolen Sexton's coat the day before and then followed him that morning, as he almost certainly did, to make sure he wasn't going to meet Cynthia Playford? You surely couldn't get more premeditated than that?"

Walsh was quiet for a few moments. "Beddoes was, I think, basically a decent sort of fellow, and as such, I'm sure he would've tried at least one more time to talk Cynthia Playford round and try to get her to give up her idea of passing on all the information she'd amassed on his great-aunt and uncle to a private investigator for follow-up." The Chief Inspector's voice was slow and deliberate. "Beddoes must've known that she'd completed her research and that she was now proposing to do something along these lines. She spoke to him over the telephone the day before she and her brother left to spend the weekend here. Mrs. Beddoes refused to confirm who phoned whom—it's only the notation in Cynthia Playford's appointment diary that says she definitely spoke to someone named Beddoes on the Thursday immediately preceding the Easter weekend. But I think he phoned her—probably one of many similar attempts I would imagine he'd made since he'd got the drift of what she was up to —and tried to get her to drop the matter. Perhaps he even threatened her with legal action . . . it would certainly explain why she suddenly parceled up all the papers connected with her research and brought them here with her to hand over to Madame . . . er, Mrs. Charles."

Walsh paused as if expecting the clairvoyante to make some comment; when she remained silent, he leaned forward and rested his folded arms on the desk.

Then, Walsh continued, "Cynthia Playford wasn't the type to threaten successfully. It would only serve to cement her resolve, though I can't see her letting that on to Beddoes. She'd string him along . . . being the type of woman she was, she'd tell him she was going away for the holiday weekend with her brother (and where they were going—somebody told Beddoes that, and my guess is that she did); and that she'd consider the matter while she was away and let him know her decision on her return, all the while knowing that she'd long since made up her mind precisely what she was going to do and had every intention of acting on it that same day. Beddoes clearly had his doubts about her promise to think things over and considered that the time had come for a more positive approach, a meeting face to face to discuss the matter—particularly in view of his state of health. He knew time was fast running out for him. And as luck would have it, when he phoned The Grand, as we now know he did, using an assumed name, Belson, on the Thursday—the same day he spoke to Cynthia Playford over the phone—to inquire about accommodation for his wife and himself for the long weekend, there'd been a cancellation; a couple who'd been going to attend the magicians' convention had dropped out at the last moment and the hotel was able to give Beddoes their room.

"Beddoes and Cynthia Playford had never met prior to that weekend. Their previous contact, again according to notes she'd made at the time in her appointment diary, had been by telephone and twice by letter. Once, very early on in the piece when she'd first begun her research, Beddoes wrote her a short letter enclosing some information she'd requested—" Walsh's eyebrows shot up. "This all started out very innocently, you know, lad," he told his sergeant, "with a simple request that Cynthia Playford had received from someone in the States to get him Amanda Beddoes's correct birth date from St. Catherine's House. And it's almost certain that hers wasn't the first approach Beddoes had had from a literary researcher about his great-aunt. However, Beddoes didn't know when she (his great-aunt) was born—no one did (this was because of a mistake about her age having been made on her death certificate). Nor did Beddoes have her place of birth, which further complicated matters; and ironically enough, he himself was delighted to have all this information when Cynthia Playford eventually turned it up . . . so delighted, in fact, that he wrote her a short thank-you note for having troubled to pass it on to him. But unfortunately—for both of them as it turned out—it didn't end there. Cynthia Playford had got hold of a tiger by the tail and she refused to let go."

Sayer asked, "Did she meet the Beddoeses—or rather, the Belsons—at the magicians' party on the Friday night? They must've all been there together in the Wellington Room at one time or another during the evening."

"Nigel Playford says not," replied Walsh. "He and his sister and the Sextons kept pretty much to themselves. But Playford was introduced to them . . . the Belsons—this was after his sister had gone up to her room and he'd returned to the party alone. But even if Beddoes had been using his real name, it wouldn't have meant anything to Playford. His sister didn't discuss her work with him; he told us that himself. Beddoes lied, of course, about not hearing anything up there on the second floor when he returned to his room after ordering sandwiches for his wife. He not only overheard Cynthia Playford arranging to meet Sexton at ten-thirty the following morning at the summit of Great Mountain, he actually saw Sexton in the doorway of her room, and Sexton saw him; and once Beddoes realised that Sexton was going to stand her up, he went in his place. The way I see it, Beddoes and Cynthia Playford met for the first time while travelling together on the cabin lift.

"Always assuming Beddoes was gentleman enough to introduce himself to her first before chucking her out," said Rhys-Williams sardonically.

"In my opinion it all happened too quickly," Walsh said meditatively, "for it to have been premeditated murder at that point in time. If they'd been higher up the mountain . . . yes, I'd be the first to agree with you that Beddoes might've set out that morning with that plan of action in mind. But she fell from the cabin only a few minutes after they'd left the landing stage. And make no mistake about it, lad, Beddoes got into that cabin with her quite by chance. It had to be that way. He had no prior knowledge that Sexton was going to back out. Sexton didn't know it himself until the very last moment. It wasn't until after Beddoes saw that Sexton wasn't going to keep his appointment with her—and as you've said, the only way he could've known this was by following Sexton that morning to see exactly where he went—that Beddoes set off after her himself and eventually caught up with her at the cabin lift where she'd had to hang about for a time because she was too early and it hadn't started running. Then at ten, when the ticket office opened, they passed through—virtually together—to the landing stage. She was a woman travelling alone, it was early and things were quiet, so she would've had every right to insist that no one—a strange man, which Beddoes still was to her; though, undoubtedly, she recognised him from the hotel—shared a cabin with her. But she made no such request. She was, I think, too preoccupied with her thoughts about Sexton and her determination to fix the magicians' contest set for the following day to care much who rode up the mountain with her. Then—" Walsh widened his eyes at Rhys-Williams "—being the gentleman I believe he was, Beddoes probably introduced himself, told her who he really was."

"And she suddenly took fright and panicked?" the sergeant asked sceptically.

Walsh shook his head. "Out of character. It would take a hell of a lot to frighten her kind. Be practically impossible, I'd say. No . . . I think he told her that her ex-boyfriend wasn't going to meet her up at the top and that he was somewhere down below wandering about on the beach. And that, I believe, is what did it. I think she was so incensed, in such a blind fury when Beddoes told her that Sexton was going to stand her up—and you'll remember what her brother and Sexton—" Walsh inclined his head at the clairvoyante "—and you, Madame, all independently of one another, told us of her behaviour the previous night and on the Saturday morning; she was definitely behaving irrationally and in an unbalanced frame of mind—that she simply forgot where she was and attempted to get out of the cabin before it went any farther and go off down to the beach in search of Sexton. She literally stepped out into fresh air. Or perhaps Beddoes even tried to restrain her (this all happened as they were approaching the first junction), they went through the junction, and somehow, while she was resisting him and they were struggling together, and just as the cabin lurched forward, she went sailing overboard."

"Yeah; and maybe, just maybe, he helped her on her way," said Rhys-Williams.

"In which case," Walsh said with a tiny smile, "I'm right, lad; it wasn't premeditated murder."

The sergeant shook his head and said, "No way. Beddoes went to a hell of a lot more trouble than you give him credit for. He knew who Sexton was . . . all about his affair with Cynthia Playford and that she was the one who'd tossed him over; and the fact that he stole Sexton's coat on the Friday morning, *before* the party that night and any gossip about Sexton and Cynthia Playford could've reached his ears—and he saw for himself the torch Sexton was still carrying for her—confirms it. Beddoes came here to Wales last weekend knowing as much about Cynthia Playford as she knew about him and his family. He deliberately set out to frame Sexton for the murder he planned to commit. And Sexton, with his idiotic behaviour on the Friday night which he then later compounded by lying to you, played right into his hands. Beddoes did *not* borrow Sexton's coat simply because it had suddenly turned a little chilly and his was upstairs in his room and Sexton's was handy, did not then forget to return it for the next twenty-four hours!"

Walsh shrugged noncommittally. Sayer, exchanging glances with the clairvoyante, rose and said, "Well, Griffith, we must be off. We've a long drive ahead of us and we hope to be home by nightfall."

Walsh stood up and shook hands again. "You're travelling back together?" he inquired, escorting them to the door.

"Yes," said Sayer. "Mrs. Charles and I are near neighbours."

Walsh gave him a quick look; dismissed the thought which entered his head as uncharitable, if not downright bitchy. Then, turning to the clairvoyante, he said, "It's been most interesting meeting you, Madame. Thank you again for all your help. I'll be honest and admit it: I almost made a terrible mistake. But then—" he smiled crookedly "—no one is infallible. We all make them . . . mistakes, don't we?" His eyes narrowed fractionally. "I understand the Sextons—Mr. *and* Mrs.—have returned safely to their home in London."

The clairvoyante looked at him steadily. "I have never once made a prediction about death or given a warning like the one concerning Mrs. Sexton which hasn't later come to pass."

Walsh grinned, unabashed. If he'd had the grace to admit he'd made a mistake, why couldn't she? He watched Sayer and the clairvoyante until they disappeared around the corner at the end of the corridor outside his office, then crossed to the window and watched them leave the building.

"Oh, by the way," said Rhys-Williams, "the unidentified male those two young spelunkers found drowned in that cave in the Swansea Valley yesterday. They've just got the medical examiner's report. It came in while you were with the Chief Constable. The victim was a hit-and-run victim. The driver of the car which ran him down paused long enough to drag him into the caves before carrying on about his business."

Walsh turned; looked mildly surprised. "He didn't drown? He was run down by a car?"

"Run *over* to be precise. Here and here—" The sergeant showed him where on his own body. "Deliberately, the medical examiner thinks. No way, he says, can he see it having been an accident—the kind one usually associates with a hit and run."

Walsh raised his eyebrows a fraction, but made no comment.

"They've also come up with a name for him."

Walsh had turned back to the window, didn't appear to be listening.

"The hit-and-run victim who wasn't a potholer after all and didn't drown in a flash flood when the river suddenly rose," the sergeant said determinedly.

Walsh looked at him over his shoulder. "So? Get on with it, lad. Why the big production? Who was he?"

"Edward Black . . . you know, as in Ted Black of Plaid-yro-Wyth, the night porter from The Grand. You did hear he'd been reported missing, didn't you? By his landlady? His bed hadn't been slept in since Saturday. He did his usual shift on Sunday night until the early a.m. of Monday morning, and then disappeared into thin air. His car's still parked in the garage out the back of The Grand." The sergeant paused. Then: "What was it you told me Sayer said about him? Didn't he say Black got that stoop of his from listening at too many keyholes?"

Walsh looked quickly out of the window, but Sayer's car had gone. His thoughts went back to the previous Monday—the flushed face and guilty, flickering eyelids; the covert look Kath Sexton had given him after they'd ridden down in the lift together; how pleased she'd been with herself about something—and his blood ran cold as the clairvoyante's prediction flashed through his mind. . . .

"There will be another death; one equally as violent as Cynthia Playford's, if not more so. Mrs. Sexton should be kept under close surveillance. . . ."

"Oh, Christ!" he murmured.

MIGNON WARNER is the author of two previous mysteries about the clairvoyante Mrs. Charles, *A Medium for Murder* and *The Tarot Murders*. She was born in Australia, but now lives in England with her husband, whom she assists in the invention, design, and manufacture of magic apparatus. She spends most of her free time pursuing her interest in psychic research and the occult. *Death in Time* is her first novel for the Crime Club.